Trapped

Children of the Apocalypse

BOOK 3

Trapped in Atlanta

R. Wesley Ibbetson

R. Wesley Ibbetson

LOOK FOR THIS PREVIOUS BOOK IN THE CHILDREN OF THE APOCALYPSE SERIES.

Trapped in Atlanta

R. Wesley Ibbetson

ACKNOWLEDGMENTS

I want to thank my family for their support in my writing efforts. I especially want to thank my wife, Patty, for her advice and patience. I also appreciate the advice my daughter, Amy, has given me on the "Children of the Apocalypse" series. She has contributed drawings and done considerable work on book covers for the series. My son, Thomas, has also helped in this effort. My son, Paul, has always been very helpful in assisting and inspiring me in the book-writing challenge.

CONTENTS

1 THE WARDEN ESCAPES..7
2 MOM AND DAD, WE ARE TRAPPED IN ATLANA............13
3 SNEAK BACK TO THE HOSPITAL.................................20
4 FOLLOWED BY THE PRISON GANG..............................25
5 BACK TO THE COMPOUND...30
6 JACOB SEES ALTANTA'S STREETS................................35
7 PRISON WARDEN...40
8 POLICE COMMISSIONER 45
9 DOCTOR'S ASSISTANT, BENNY ROBINSON..................50
10 SUSIE, THE WAITRESS..56
11 SETTLING IN...62
12 JUDY'S PROGRESS..67
13 MOLINE COUNCIL MEETS..73
14 NO-WAY BART..79
15 FREE BREAD...85

16 GANG HEADQUARTERS	90
17 OUTSIDE THE GATE	96
18 KILLER DOG PACK	103
19 REMEMBER OUR PACT	110
20 TERRORIST CONNECTION	117
21 CINNAMON ROLLS	123
22 MILITARY RESCUE	129
23 GOODBYE GANG, HELLO MOB	135
24 THE BAD EGGS ARE BROKEN	141
HOW TO DECIPHER THE CODE	146
COMING SOON, BOOK 4, ESCAPE FROM ATLANTA	148
BOOK 4, CONTENTS	149
BOOK 4, CHAPTER 1, WE ARE GOING HOME	151
BOOK 4, CHAPTER 2, GETTING OUT OF ATLANTA— OR NOT	157
BOOK 4, CHAPTER 8, BART'S HOSTAGE	164

Chapter 1

The Warden Escapes

Before the Robinson kids arrived at Ezra's place in Atlanta, the prison gang got their chance to escape. They had been waiting for the solar pulse to remove the prison guards. When the pulse hit, their vehicles wouldn't start, and their cell phones wouldn't work. The correctional facility employees began to be affected immediately. Some lived clear across Atlanta.

The guards working at the time had no way to go home. A few who lived close were allowed to leave and walk home. The remaining men who continued to work became fatigued, and it became necessary to start rotating sleep periods.

The Warden was aware of the solar pulse and that the situation was not likely to be fixed any time soon. He initially kept this information to himself. This knowledge was a heavy load for him to carry. He knew that soon none of his workers would report to work. The food would run out. The diesel stored to run the backup generator would go dry. The prison warden dreaded thinking about the decision he would have to make when that day came. Would he walk away and leave the inmates to die in their cells, or would he turn them loose on Atlanta? One of the prisoners seemed to know that the Warden would have to make that decision. This prisoner was one of the known terrorists. His name was Genghis Lee.

When the Warden checked the cells, Genghis looked at him and sneered, "Warden, you know that a solar pulse has fried everything? You and I know that this problem is not going to get fixed quickly. When the food is all gone and your standby generator runs out of fuel, are you going to walk away and leave us locked up here to rot?"

The Warden paused for a long moment, then jerked around and walked off without commenting. Two of Genghis' buddies laughed, and one of them screamed at the Warden. "What are you going to do, Warden? If you are going to let us out, do it now. If you leave us in here to rot, we will get out anyway, and we will hunt you down and kill you." Again, the inmate laughed, his disrespectful laugh. He yelled, "We will get you, Warden!" The inmate looked at Genghis, "How long are we gonna wait before we break out?"

"I don't think it's quite time yet. There are still too many guards around. Our outside people will decide when to come and take over. The guards will not show up when the food and power run out." Genghis' friend again laughed his hysterical laugh.

The big leader of the 'lifers' had joined Genghis and his friend. "I hear they're going to reduce our food allowances this evening. There aren't any food trucks coming into Atlanta. Everything is totally shutdown, just like you said it would be. I don't know how you knew, but I guess it doesn't matter. We're going to get out of here soon."

Genghis chuckled, "I'll let you know when our outside people are coming. Get your people ready. We will get out of here and go into the city and get everything we need to control it. It may happen tomorrow."

More and more of the guards were leaving. They were hearing stories about looting and home robberies happening. These men were worried about their families at home. The Warden knew that when these men left, they would never be back. The food supplies were low, and the diesel would probably run out soon. The Warden thought that tomorrow would be a decision day. He was thinking about this when his wife showed up. The Warden was surprised and concerned that she had walked all the way to the prison.

The Warden's wife embraced him, exclaiming, "It is crazy out there. Do you know what has caused this?"

"Yes, come into my private office." He shut the door and locked it. "The government confidentially told me this solar pulse was coming. All electronics are fried and won't get fixed soon. Did you get plenty of food stocked up at home like I asked you to?"

"Yes, but I was so frustrated because you wouldn't tell me why I needed to. Now, I see why."

"Yes, I promised the government that I wouldn't tell anyone what was coming. I think it would have caused a lot of panic."

"Now that it's too late, people are running out of everything. The stores are all being looted. I saw a lot of desperate looking people as I came here. I'm worried about going home."

"Wait! Let me think, maybe we can go home together. We are almost out of food and diesel here. I was thinking about leaving tomorrow. Now, maybe we could leave during the night. I can tell the few guards that are left here I have a very difficult decision to make. Should I leave the inmates locked in the prison? It makes me feel like a failure, but I also think it would be a failure to turn all these criminals loose on the residents of Atlanta. After the evening meal, I'll get the remaining guards together. I'll ask them what they think we should do. When you and I leave, we will take guns with us."

The evening meal finished most of the food that was in the prison. The inmates were chanting and complaining about the reduction in food. The Warden called the remaining guards in for a meeting. He explained to them about the solar pulse. He praised them. "Thank you, men, for your loyalty and steadfast work ethic. I know you and your families have sacrificed to keep this prison operating these past few days. It may be time to leave and walk home to our families. My wife has come here to check on me. I hate to send her back by herself. We will take guns with us, and you should too. I have questions for you. Do you think we should leave tonight and should we leave the inmates locked in the prison? We may never come back here again. We may not survive the winter here in Atlanta. It will be terrible with no food, water or power in the city. Atlanta will disintegrate. We might want to try to get out of Atlanta. Anyway, let's go to the pantry and find what food is left that we can lay out for each of you to take."

One of the guards spoke, "Go to the pantry and lay out the food. We will get answers to your questions."

"My wife and I will be in the pantry laying out some food for each of you." The Warden's wife smiled and took her husband's arm.

The pantry was nearly cleaned out. The Warden and his wife started making piles for each of them. They were looking for some bags to put the food in when the guards returned.

"We have an answer to your questions, Warden. We are very willing to leave tonight. The other question is harder. We had to consider letting murders loose on Atlanta or being murders ourselves. Our decision was…."

Suddenly, a security alarm sounded. They all moved to a nearby window where they could see the prison entrance. A dozen heavily armed men were approaching the front gate. The Warden paused and announced, "Our decision doesn't matter now. It may be a good time to leave by the back exit."

Chapter 2

Mom and Dad, We Are Trapped in Atlanta

Tom Robinson and David Billman had driven into Atlanta in an old 1960 Chevy 2-ton farm truck. This old truck had no modern computer electronics controls, so it would still run after the large solar EMP pulse hit the earth and destroyed all electronics. The pulse created an apocalyptic situation in America that trapped Tom's uncle and his wife in the rapidly deteriorating city of Atlanta. Tom and David had driven the old truck into the city to bring Tom's Uncle John and his wife, Carol, out of the spiraling chaos of Atlanta. Tom's Uncle John was a medical doctor interning at a hospital in Atlanta. Tom had been unaware that his sister Susie and his brother Benny had stowed away in the back of the old grain truck. Upon entering the city, a gang of escaped prisoners attacked them. They were now held up in a gated community created by an ingenious man named Ezra. David and the kids survived the prison gang attack but now felt trapped and unable to leave Atlanta because of the prison gang.

Tom and David had brought a load of farm-stored grains and some flour that they ground from wheat stored at David Billman's farm. Today, the Robinson kids ate their breakfast at Ezra's hidden restaurant. They enjoyed some specialty bread made from the flour they had risked their lives to bring into Atlanta. Now, it was clear to them that they were trapped in Ezra's place. The prison gang that had nearly killed them when they came into Atlanta made it unsafe for them to leave. Susie had even brought up the question about whether they would be safe while waiting in Ezra's compound.

Ezra's sister sent a runner to Jacob, who had been assigned to take care of the Robinson kids' needs. He arrived and asked, "How can I help you today? Ezra sends his regards. He regrets that you have been caught in this delay. He does, however, appreciate having Doctor John here at this time."

Tom greeted Jacob. "How are things looking for our safe return to David Billman's place? We didn't anticipate staying when we left yesterday. We thought we would be back at David's place last night. Now that we know about this prison gang, please keep us up to date on how this problem is being handled."

"Okay," Jacob replied. "I see you all are carrying the CBs that I got you last night. I will give you my channel number, then you can reach me anytime. You may be here for a while, so I will tell you about things you might like to do while you are detained. We have two shooting ranges and a school that has just started. We can visit about these later. Who knows how long it's going to take to resolve this problem? Can you stay here at the café for a while? Your Uncle John is in a meeting close by. I will see if he can get free to come and see you this morning.

Tom and the kids were pleased to hear this. Tom replied, "Susie and I will finish our meal, and then maybe have another cup of coffee."

Benny rubbed his stomach and announced, "I'm stuffed. There's a limit to how much coffee I can drink."

Susie declared, "Benny! You better not drink any coffee."

"Well then, I am ready to take a nap. I hope John comes to visit soon."

Tom laughed, "Oh, Susie, go ahead and give him some coffee."

"No!" Susie yelled. Tom, and even Benny, laughed.

John and Carol walked up at that moment. "I see that you're having a good time," John observed. "I am pleased to see that. Carol and I have been wanting to apologize for getting you into this mess. We were so grateful that you and your dad offered us this hope of a way out of the city during this apocalypse. Now, it looks like Ezra is going to try to persuade us to stay here and work for him. Right now, he certainly needs us. Just the thought of staying makes me feel guilty for having asked you to come for us. We have caused you to become trapped here and have delayed your travel back home."

That statement triggered Benny, "Yeah! We should be traveling every day. Winter will come before we get home."

John and Carol both told Bennie they were sorry. Benny suddenly noticed that John looked a lot like his dad. This resemblance made him homesick, but it also made him feel warmer toward his uncle. Benny thought he would lighten up the situation a little, so he said, "Oh well, I guess I'll just have another cup of coffee."

"No, you won't!" Susie insisted.

Tom laughed and added, "Well, John, you were in a terribly dangerous situation, and none of us knew anything about Ezra's medical facility and his need for your services. We should wait and see what happens and hope for the best."

John thanked Tom for looking at it that way. "Carol and I and the other medical staff are waiting for Ezra to return from talking to his military general. They are considering letting some of us go back to the hospital and rescue about three patients I left there. We would also grab some more supplies. I would like to bring those patients here where I could take care of them. I am a little worried that Ezra and the general might be formulating a plan to use us as bait to get some of the prison gang. That might put us at extra risk."

Tom acknowledged that he also wondered at times if he might be a pawn in a bigger plan, but he reminded himself that his dad trusted Ezra. "I trust Ezra, John, because my dad trusts him. I feel that we are in good hands."

"Very good," John returned. "We better get back to our meeting room and wait for Ezra to return." He looked at Benny, "Benny, my boy, you go easy on that coffee. The old saying is 'it can stunt your growth.'" He gave Benny a warm hug and waved goodbye to Tom and Susie.

Benny had tears in his eyes. He finally blurted out, "Let's go call Mom and Dad."

"Yes," Tom agreed, "Let's go back to our room and give them a call."

The Robinson kids got their mother on their ham radio on their first try. She asked, "Is that you, kids?"

"Yes," they all replied. "Where are you, Mom?"

"I'm out at the farm. We were a little worried since you didn't call last night. Is everything alright?"

"Well, yes and no, Mom," Tom answered. "We're all physically okay, but the bad news is, we're trapped in Atlanta. We think we're safe at Ezra's place, but it's not safe to try to leave, and we don't know how long it'll be before it'll be safe to leave."

"Oh no!" their mother's voice echoed loudly over the radio. "Let me go get your dad."

"Where is dad?" Tom asked.

"He's just out here in the cornfield. He's close by. I'll be right back."

The kids' dad got to the phone. "Your mom tells me you are trapped in Atlanta. She says you may be there for a while. Tell me about it." Tom filled him in on what had taken place. Benny told him about his sister, "the shooter," rescuing all of them.

Peter acknowledged, "It looks like maybe I was wrong about asking Susie and you, Benny, to stay behind at the Billman's. Also, I am disappointed about the prison gang and that John and Carol might change their minds about leaving Atlanta."

Tom asked his dad what he was doing out in the cornfield.

"Picking field corn. We have to recognize potential food since there will be no food restocking of grocery stores. The renter, who planted the corn, and I were handpicking wheelbarrow loads of ears of corn. This corn was planted late and still is a little too mature for eating off the cob but is about right to cut off the cob to preserve in canning jars. It doesn't taste as good as sweet corn, but it is food. The renter's family is here to share in this project. They don't know we have a hidden place to live out here. You kids, call us every day and keep us updated. Goodbye, and God bless."

Chapter 3

Sneak Back to the Hospital

Ezra returned to meet with the hospital staff. He spoke to all of them, saying, "You are too important to put at much risk. We talked about using you to draw out the prison gang, but we decided to do just the opposite. We will sneak you in and out. We will only risk sending in two of you. Dr. John will have to go because he knows where the patients are, and they know him. The hospital administrator will be the other medical person going. He has made a list of what we need from the hospital. We will not use cars to transport you. The prison gang always seems attracted to moving automobiles.

"You will be camouflaged as scavengers. We will send you there in two groups of three. John, you will have two soldiers with you, and the administrator will have two soldiers with him. You will go in separate groups. We have already sent a surveillance team in that direction. I think the sooner we do this, the better. These patients you had to leave, John, surely need attention as soon as possible. The other thing is, we may be in a war with this prison gang before long. The general is planning a distraction for when you are ready to leave the hospital. The advance surveillance team has a person that will try to hotwire an ambulance. He will try to bypass all the computers in the ambulance. If this doesn't work, we will send vehicles for you."

Ezra announced, "I am going to our newly established 'War Room' that is being set up to monitor all soldiers that are out in the city. Jacob will get the groups dressed as scavengers."

Jacob told John and the administrator to come with him. He said, "We have a team working on these disguises in a special room. I want the rest of you to go to the medical facility and prepare for anything that might happen. If I get a chance, I will start scheduling our people to get health exams from Dr. John when he gets back."

R. Wesley Ibbetson

The camouflage room was a busy place. A lot of runners were being prepared and sent out. There was a case of Israeli-made Uzis on the floor. Each of the runners concealed one of these weapons under a ragged jacket. They smeared John's face to look like he needed to shave and needed to wash off some dirt. He had a bag that contained usable things like small bottles of water, breakfast bars, and a first aid kit. He had an empty two-liter pop bottle tied to his belt. The administrator was equipped the same way. They soon were ready to begin their journey to the hospital. The advanced surveillance team did not see any problems yet. One of John's soldiers moved out ahead, and the other one walked beside John. John thought the pace was pretty fast. Occasionally, they would slow down and try to look like they were doing a little scavenging. John was anxious to get to the hospital to see if the patients he left were still alive and if he could rescue them. He thought this opportunity to save them happened quickly after he mentioned it to Ezra. He was hopeful that he could bring help to these injured men.

John and his soldiers saw hoards of desperate-looking people wandering about the streets. John noticed that some people would look at his empty two-liter bottle tied to his waist. Not seeing anything in his bottle, they would shuffle off. One man asked him where he was going to get water. John told him that he had heard there was a stream about three blocks ahead close to the hospital. As they approached the hospital, they could see the stream that John knew was there. Now, they could see a lot of people gathered along its banks.

The scavenger had followed behind John. When he saw this stream of water, he moved ahead of John and his soldier and headed toward it. John and his soldier turned on a paved road and went over a bridge toward the hospital's back door. The front soldier dropped back and told them he had gotten a message from the advance team telling them it was clear to come in the back entrance of the hospital. They passed the man who was working on an ambulance. He asked them to let him know when they were close to being ready to leave. If he was not progressing in getting the ambulance to run, he would call Ezra to send cars.

The back door of the hospital was open. John figured they had left it open when they had run out a few days earlier. He also assumed that many people had gone in and out that door after he had passed through it. As John entered this time, he noticed a dank, musty smell. Two runners went ahead of John and checked the entrance area with their guns ready for whatever. They waited for John and the administrator to lead the way. The administrator took three of the advanced team to help him gather equipment and supplies and bring them to the back door, ready to carry out.

John told his two soldiers and one advanced team member to get wheelchairs and follow him. He was saddened to see how the hospital had been trashed and was concerned about the smell of decaying bodies. John expected this, but he couldn't help but worry about the patients he had come to help. He kept pointing the way, and one of the soldiers was always up front and checking each turn. They had already moved past several scavengers. The scavengers were anxious to avoid men with guns.

John's heart began racing as they entered the room of the first patient he had come to get. John saw that the man was still in his bed, but he didn't see any movement from the man as they entered his room.

Chapter 4

Followed by the Prison Gang

John hurried over to the bed of his former patient, Ben Grady, who hadn't moved since they arrived. John reached out and touched his shoulder and looked at his face. Ben was looking directly at him. Suddenly, there was a moment of recognition. Ben raised up, saying, "Dr. John, it is you! I can't believe what I am seeing! People come in here all the time looking for anything they can use. I always play dead, and they never know the difference. I probably smell pretty much like the dead people also. I don't know."

"Ben," John queried, "Are you stronger? We want to take you out of here!"

"Yes!" Ben yelled as he sat up and swung his legs over the edge of the bed.

"Wait," a soldier said as he brought up a wheelchair. They put Ben in it and quickly moved out. The soldier said he would take Ben down to the back door. John directed the rest of the soldiers to move down the hallway to his next patient. When they opened his door, they found him sitting on his bed, and he had a wheelchair beside it. It appeared that he had been doing some exploring. It didn't take long to get him in the wheelchair and out the door. He was already familiar with moving himself around in a wheelchair. Another soldier went with him to the exit waiting area. John told the soldier to tell the ambulance mechanic that they were getting close to being ready to leave.

John directed his remaining soldier to his third potential recovery patient. John was hopeful that he was okay, and they could move right along in getting him also.

John found him in his room, and he was moving a little bit. As John approached him, the patient looked at him and said, "Boy, you are a sight for sore eyes."

"Are you alright?"

The man replied, "No, I'm not! I haven't had any water or food for about a day and a half. Some guy found my stash and took it. I think I'm dehydrated, and I don't feel good."

John got his backpack off and gave him a bottle of water. He drank it and said that he felt better but was still thirsty. "I have been extremely hot in this closed-up hospital with no air conditioning."

The soldier got him in a wheelchair and took him down to the back exit door waiting area. The hospital administrator was still gathering supplies. He indicated that he was about ready, also. John told one of the runners to notify the man working on the ambulance that they were ready to leave. One of the soldiers asked the three waiting patients if any of the scavengers looked like an escaped prisoner.

Two of John's patients indicated that some of the scavengers looked like they had on prison uniforms. John knew this was important information for Ezra. This thought was sidelined when a soldier came in and told them that the ambulance was running and had pulled up close to load. They decided to load the hospital equipment and supplies first. There was barely room for the patients after the supplies were loaded. Two of the soldiers squeezed in for the ride. They packed in tight. Some of the soldiers would walk back to the compound.

The ambulance did not go too far before the driver got a call from Ezra. "I just got a report from one of my runners that the ambulance is being followed. Try delaying them for a while: take them on a wild goose chase. Give us a little time to set up a shoulder-fired missile to wipe out their car. We will tell you when and where to lead them past it." The ambulance driver acknowledged that he would.

He looked at John and a soldier that was close to John. "You heard that message, didn't you?" They nodded that they had.

The driver reduced his speed slightly and turned off on a side street that led away from the compound. They traveled straight for a while. Suddenly, John saw a car far back behind them. The sight of the vehicle gave John a chill. He was afraid they intended to learn where the ambulance was going. Some group must have been watching the hospital, anticipating people with cars to return. They had obviously targeted this group (Ezra's group). Ezra's soldiers had wiped out members of a raiding group that had targeted the hospital earlier. Some of these raiders may have escaped and reported that some people left the hospital in cars. The leaders of these raiders probably realized that the people with vehicles and interest in the hospital were a significant group. In today's world, this group stood out. The raiders were probably the prison gang.

Ezra's General called the driver and told him to keep going for six more blocks, and there would be a surprise waiting there. They had only gone two blocks when John noticed the car behind them pull over to the side of the road and stop. He was surprised to see this happen. Then, when they had gone two more blocks, they passed a car with a man standing behind it. He had a shoulder-fired weapon aimed at the car that had stopped. As soon as the ambulance went by, the soldier fired. The missile blew up the pursuer's car. John wondered how Ezra had gotten these missiles and, more importantly, how he knew to set them up closer than what he reported to them. It appeared that Ezra may have been thinking that the prison gang was listening to his radio messages.

The ambulance driver stopped and backed up. There were two soldiers; one stood by with an AR-15. Ezra told the ambulance driver that he was clear to head directly back to the compound. They were now a long way from there. There were a lot of stalled cars to maneuver around on their way back. John checked on his patients. The dehydrated man was still not feeling very well.

Chapter 5

Back to the Compound

The ambulance pulled through a storefront garage door. The sign above the door said, 'Auto Brakes Specialist.' Inside, they pulled up to the emergency medical facility entrance. The nursing staff came out with gurneys to get John's patients. John's patient, Ben Grady, looked at John, smiling, and said, "It took a while to get here, but what a place you have, Doc. How did this happen? I see that someone even left the lights on for us. Is this Motel 6?"

John smiled back, "Strange things do occasionally occur. We will just count our blessings."

Ben acknowledged, "I definitely am doing that. I never dreamed that I would be this fortunate."

The administrator and a soldier were unloading the hospital equipment and supplies. Ezra showed up with his general. "We want to question the three patients about the prison people they saw at the hospital," Ezra announced. He looked at the ambulance. "I think we'll leave this ambulance that runs here at our medical facility."

John asked Ezra and the general about the trap for the pursuing car. "I was expecting that trap to be several blocks on down the road. Those renegades seemed to get spooked and stopped following well short of where you said you would get them."

"Yes," the general answered. "We assumed this sophisticated gang may be monitoring our CB communications. So, we set up our trap well ahead of where we said it would be. They spooked so quickly, we almost didn't get them. Now we know that we have a whole new problem of communications. We will have to do something about that. I am calling our command center right now and telling them to inform all our people about this breach. We need to stop all communications now!"

Ezra spoke to one of his runners, "Go to the command center and tell them to start working to encrypt our messages so that they are not understandable. We will have to develop a codebook for our people and put it into effect tomorrow. We need to work on some other approaches. I am sending a runner to the police commissioner and the commissioner of prisons. I don't know these people, but it is time to get acquainted. We need to learn all we can about this prison gang."

John, Ezra, and the general went into the medical facility where John's patients had been made comfortable. John immediately began checking each of the patients. After John finished his examinations, Ezra and the general began their questioning. The patients were able to provide a good description of the hospital raiders. Ezra and the general then went back to the command center.

John and the administrator sorted out all of the supplies and equipment they had retrieved from the abandoned hospital. The equipment would expand their testing and treating capabilities at Ezra's medical facility. The resident nurse told John, "There are three people from our community who want to see a doctor. I'm also going to start scheduling our people for wellness visits, if that's okay with you. Ezra wants to get everyone on a healthful wellness plan. Maybe we can start now while you are trapped here dealing with this prison gang. I guess we don't know how long you'll be here. I'm sure you'll be well compensated."

John agreed that he was willing to provide this service. "I'm here, and I might as well stay busy."

The Robinson kids had rested after visiting with their parents. Benny took a nap after his big breakfast. Later, Tom and Susie voiced their concerns about Uncle John traveling back to his former hospital. As the day wore on, the kids decided to go to the medical facility and see if he had made it back yet. They knew they could call Jacob and find out. The kids were also antsy to get out and move around, and Tom knew how to find the medical facility. The kids stopped by David's room and got him to go with them.

The resident nurse was at the entrance desk. Tom asked her, "Has our Uncle John returned from the hospital trip?"

"Yes, they are back successfully, and your uncle is now with a patient. I'll have him come out and see you as soon as he's finished."

The kids saw a few other people in the waiting room. Tom thought, "They've taken over Uncle John. They have gotten him working for them already."

A short time later, John smiled at the kids and gave each of them a hug. Tom spoke up, "We've been worried about you and wanted to check and see if you had made it back safely."

John reflected with a frown. "We did have a scare coming back. We were pursued by a car probably belonging to the prison gang. The soldiers were able to blow up the car. It now appears they have been monitoring our CB messages. They are a pretty sophisticated enemy. This problem they present is going to take some time to resolve. For now, we just need to hunker down and wait this out. Normally, we can call Jacob and find out the latest. However, we are not supposed to use our CBs right now."

Tom groaned, "This gang is a problem to all of us for sure. We are so glad that you got back safely. We better let you get back to work."

John replied, "Thanks for checking on me."

As they walked off, Tom asked David, "Would you like to come over to our room and get on our ham radio and call Kathy and see if she will answer? We left our ham radio at your place. If Kathy doesn't answer it, Judy probably will when she gets back from Moline tonight."

Chapter 6

Jacob Sees Atlanta's Streets

Tom told David, "We said we would call the ham radio that we left at your place when we got to our room. Can you see if you can get Kathy to answer? Don't give Kathy or Judy's last name or the name of Moline. Don't mention the bakery or the name 'prison gang.' We can refer to these things without specifically naming them. We'll know what we're talking about."

When they got to the Robinson kids' room, Tom dialed the call and gave the microphone to David. David tried calling out to Kathy, urging her to answer. There was no answer. Tom reminded them, "Judy will be home in a few hours. We will try again then."

Ezra gave Jacob the prison warden's address and asked Jacob to find him. On his way out of the compound, he stopped to talk to Tom and David. "I'm going on a mission to find the prison warden and get information from him. I'll not be available to you until I come back. Don't try to call me while I'm out there. I'm not a runner, but Ezra needs someone who could make a deal with the warden if there is an opportunity." Jacob was wearing a backpack, and it looked nearly full. One of Ezra's runners, a soldier, was going with him. Jacob asked Tom if he would ask Dr. John to refrain from calling him.

"I'll be glad to tell him. We wish you success and a safe return."

Tom and the kids again headed for the medical facility. David went along with them. As they visited with John, they felt hopeful that Jacob would find the warden and get useful information from him.

Jacob had not been on the streets since the pulse. He was shocked and somewhat scared by what he saw. The condition of the people was disturbing to Jacob. Jacob and the soldier moved along as quickly as Jacob could go. It was not too long before they smelled something. They saw a dead body in an alley. It looked like someone might have dragged this older person out of his house. Jacob thought to himself, "I wonder if an older couple might have lost a spouse. The remaining spouse may have only been able to drag the body out of the house a short distance. I don't see any sign of foul play. This person may have starved or run out of water or medication. Similar things might be happening all over the city. Younger people would have gone out searching for water and food. Some would have heard about Ezra's free water. Others might find a stream or some source of water. Food sources will be quickly disappearing."

Jacob tried to stop thinking about the misery that he was seeing, but the moment's reality was too compelling. "How fortunate the people of my compound are. We're not even a drop in the bucket compared to all of these people who have nothing."

Jacob knew his good fortune was the result of Ezra's foresight. He hoped that the plans they were making to produce food would work. The bakery was the closest of the projects. Egg production would be a lifesaver. The success of these projects would only bring relief to a relatively small number of people. Still, Jacob thought these projects were a step in the right direction because some people would benefit.

Jacob had some sense of satisfaction when he thought about the four small loaves of bread in his backpack. Other small items also might be potentially convincing in this time of scarcity. One might call these negotiable items. Jacob and the soldier had already had to defend their backpacks. Twice, aggressive men had told them to hand them over. Both times, Jacob's soldier had waved his gun at them, and they decided to move on.

Finally, Jacob and his soldier arrived at their destination. They knocked loudly many times before someone finally yelled, "Alright! What do you want?"

"We want to talk to the prison warden," Jacob answered and gave his name.

The man yelled back, "He's not here."

"We have gifts for him or anybody who can take us to him."

The man was silent.

Jacob repeated, "We have gifts! Come and look at them!"

"What kind of gifts?"

"Food and water, plus other things."

A man slowly appeared from a side door. "Let me see what ya got."

Jacob reached in his pack and pulled out a bottle of water, a Snicker's bar, a loaf of bread, and a container of pepper spray.

The man took a long look at the items, then looked up at them, "What do you want with the warden?"

"We want to talk to him and give him these gifts, or we can give these gifts to anyone who can take us to him. Can you take us to him?"

"Yeah, but why would I?"

Jacob handed him a bottle of water. The man grabbed it and drank it immediately. Jacob started to give him the candy bar but quickly withdrew it. "Take us to the warden, and you can have plenty more."

The man hesitated, then muttered, "Okay, if you let me eat the candy bar on the way."

Chapter 7

Prison Warden

The man at the warden's house quickly ate the candy bar Jacob had given him. The man whined, "You aren't going to get me in trouble, are you? I'm supposed to screen people looking for the warden, but you guys don't look like former inmates."

Jacob assured him that he was right. "We are just out trying to do good."

The man whined again, "That's what everybody says, but most people don't have anything to bribe me with, so I usually have to end up leading them into a trap."

Jacob was alarmed but immediately responded, "Well, I hope they were all escaped prisoners."

The man looked at Jacob and finally admitted, "I think most of them were." This reply didn't put Jacob at ease.

Jacob told the man that he did not require that the warden expose himself to them, "We want to be close enough to hear him and be able to talk to him."

"Okay," the man agreed, "I won't have him come out; he can stay inside and talk to you." They came to a building that looked more like a warehouse than a dwelling. The man yelled, "This is Derryl! I have two men here offering gifts, and they want to talk to you. You can stay inside; they say they don't need to see you."

Some man inside yelled back, "Who have you brought to see me, Derryl?"

Derryl asked, "Who are you guys?"

Jacob answered, "I'm Jacob; I'm a messenger from a man you may know named Ezra. He is a pawn shop owner and communications operator—more importantly, he is a provider of a self-sustaining community that has food, water, electricity, and security. My partner with me is one of Ezra's soldiers. He is retired military. I tell you all this because I believe your man, Derryl, is not lying to me, and I trust you are the warden."

A man walked into view and asked, "Why would you want to talk to the warden?"

Jacob answered, "We believe a gang of escaped prisoners are operating in Atlanta. We want to learn everything there is to know about these escapees so we can eliminate them and stop the damage they are doing."

"Come into my warehouse; I have heard of this guy Ezra." The warehouse was mostly bare, but a few chairs were visible. "Please sit down," the man said.

Derryl asked, "Do you have any more bottles of water?" The soldier produced several bottles from his backpack; Jacob was thirsty from the long, fast walk and got a bottle for himself.

After taking a couple of sips, he asked Derryl's man, "You are the prison warden, aren't you?"

"Yes, I am."

"You are aware of the existence of this prison gang, aren't you?" Derryl and the warden both confirmed that they were.

The warden explained, "That's why I'm hiding out; these escaped prisoners are trying to find me, and they'll kill me if they do." Jacob had noticed that both Derryl and the warden wore sidearms. "So," the warden continued, "you say you would like to eliminate them? That sounds gutsy, don't you think?"

"Yes," Jacob responded, "They're interfering with our operations and attacking our vehicles whenever we send them out. We've been destroying their vehicles with our shoulder-fired missile launchers. Our operations are now on hold until we can learn more about them. We need to know the location of their headquarters and the names of their leaders. Psychological profiles of their leaders might be helpful. We want to know where they got their equipment to communicate. They are able to coordinate their operations and listen to our communications."

The warden stopped Jacob. "I can provide you some of this information, but what are these operations that you refer to?"

"I mentioned our community of people. We are trying to supply our essential needs and make these available to as many people as possible." Jacob reached into his pack and pulled out one of his small loaves of bread. "We're attempting to set up a bakery in a town about 50 miles from here. Ezra has a farmer who is grinding wheat into flour. He recently brought a truckload of farm grains and sacks of flour to us. Even with our escort, the gang attacked him. We sent a large government surplus electrical generator to the bakery town, and the convoy was attacked as it left Atlanta. We hoped to get egg and broiler production going."

"I get the picture; I'm impressed. It sounds like you have vehicles that run and soldiers with some firepower. You also have a lot of ambition."

Jacob set the loaf of bread on the table. The warden reached out, picked it up, and sniffed it. He tore off a piece and tasted it. He gave a piece of bread to Derryl, who quickly ate it. The warden stood up and took the rest of the bread through a door. He returned without it. "I'd like to take you to a friend of mine who can probably answer more of your questions."

As they stood up, a lady entered the room smiling. "Thank you for the delicious bread!"

Jacob responded, "You're welcome." He handed her another loaf. The warden introduced her as his wife.

Derryl spoke up, "Where are the rest of the gifts you promised me?"

"Oh yes," Jacob responded, and he took the remaining gifts from his backpack and handed them to Derryl.

The warden was anxious to leave. "I want to take you to my friend, the police commissioner."

Chapter 8

Police Commissioner

The warden looked at Jacob and said, "If we are walking, I want to get my AR-15 and get one for Derryl. I believe your soldier has one under his jacket. It is not too far to my friend's house." He joined them at the door with the guns. The warden led the way, with Derryl close behind him. Jacob and his soldier followed. Jacob noticed that the warden and Derryl were alert, and they kept scanning the area as they walked. Jacob's nose again warned him before they saw a couple of bodies. These men had been shot. Jacob's group kept walking as if the bodies were not there.

They came to an upper-class home. The warden gave a special knock on the door. Someone inside checked the peephole and then opened the door. A man stood there holding a long gun. He looked around and then motioned for them to come in. They were seated, and the warden introduced them and explained why they were there. The mention of a prison gang noticeably perked the man's interest.

He looked at Jacob, saying, "So, you have an agenda to neutralize this prison gang? This gang's very powerful and sophisticated. They raided my police headquarters and got most of our communication devices. Now, they're hunting for my friend, the warden. The government warned us that the pulse was coming. We had to keep it a secret, but we put all our communication devices in Faraday cages to protect them from the magnetic pulse. Then, after the pulse, we had no transportation, and soon, no one showed up for work. At some point, the prison was opened. The gang was ready with plans. They hit the police station the same day they escaped. I think they hit us first and got our communications equipment and stored weapons. Antique vehicles were their next target. Being mobile and partially armed prepared them to start looting the gun shops. Finally, the food warehouses were raided. These people are smart and organized."

Jacob broke in, "Do you have any of these personal radios? Have you tried to listen in on their conversations? I'd like to get one of these units for our War Room. This would give us a distinct advantage over them."

"Sure, I'll get you one."

"Good!" Jacob exclaimed. "Would you be willing to come to our compound and strategize with us? You could shop in our grocery store and have a meal in our restaurant. You could even visit our doctor if you wanted to."

"I'm ready and willing to come without the extra enticement. It sounds a lot like Christmas," chuckled the warden.

"I'll get one of our communication devices, and I'll be ready to go," the police chief replied. "Three of us can ride on my antique motorcycle."

"I'm a runner, so I can run all the way to our compound," announced Jacob's soldier. "I will start ahead of you and watch for potential trouble."

The police chief went to get one of their radios. He came back and said, "Follow me to my garage." In the garage was the big, beautiful, antique motorcycle. The chief proudly declared, "It runs! I have used it several times since the pulse." Jacob noticed that he had an AR-15 strapped on it.

Derryl waved to them, saying, "I would like to go to your compound sometime in the future."

The big cycle purred to life. Jacob directed their travel and watched for his runner. They traveled fairly fast until they caught up with him. The riders had to dodge around stalled cars and crowds of people begging for food. They finally spotted Jacob's runner in front of a small, older house. An old weak-looking couple was sitting on the front porch. This couple had a sign which read, "We are old. We need food and water." The runner had his pack off and had handed each of them a water bottle and a breakfast bar. The moment the cycle stopped, the warden popped off and brought up his AR-15.

The runner immediately had his pack back on and sprinted off. The police chief waited a moment as the older couple tried to say thank you to the rapidly disappearing runner. The old folks wisely hurried back into their house before someone came along and took this life-saving gift away. Jacob heard locks clicking in their door. The police chief moved off rapidly to find the runner again.

Jacob warned the chief, "We're approaching my headquarters. We've set up a barricade on this street. My runner will have the gate open for us, but I will step off and show myself when we get there." The chief nodded that he understood.

When they approached the gate, it was wide open, and a man with a gun was waving them to come on through. Once inside the entrance, Jacob got off the cycle. The man there had instructions for him. "Go to the restaurant; your advanced runner will be there with Ezra."

Ezra and another man were waiting for them when they got to the restaurant. Ezra greeted them and told Jacob, "Good job! We're glad you're back safely with these men."

Jacob introduced the men to Ezra. "I'm pleased to meet you," smiled Ezra as he shook their hands. "I appreciate your coming. I'll try to make your stay as comfortable as possible.

"First things first! I understand that you have a radio device that the prison gang may be using in their operations. Could I have my general take this radio and start monitoring them immediately? We might learn about some operation they are planning that might endanger us."

Chapter 9

Doctor's Assistant, Benny Robinson

The police chief got the radio out of his pocket. He showed the general how it worked.

The general stated, "If it is okay with you, I'll take this radio to our command center and start monitoring it. I will probably see you there later."

The chief wished him good luck.

Ezra led them into the restaurant. He asked them if they were hungry. It was a little past midafternoon, so the warden answered, "Maybe later," and the chief agreed with him. Ezra suggested that maybe they would like to pick up some coffee and go to the command center and talk about what they could do about the prison gang. The two men agreed to that.

As they passed through the restaurant, Jacob saw the Robinsons and David having an afternoon Pepsi. Jacob told Ezra that he would catch up with them later. Benny stood when he saw Jacob. Benny knew that Jacob had stopped by earlier and told them that he was going out of the compound onto the Atlanta streets on a mission to find the prison warden. The Robinson kids had speculated, hopefully, that Jacob would be successful. They hoped that the gang could be dealt with soon, and they would be free to get on their way home.

Benny smiled at Jacob. "I see you made it back and brought two men with you. Is one of them the warden?"

"Yes," Jacob answered, "and the other man's his friend, the police chief. They're both interested in trying to help us deal with the prison gang. So, Benny, I am encouraged by this. Everything we can learn about this gang may help shorten the time it takes to deal with them. I'm sure it's going to be at least a few days before it will be safe for you to leave. We need to think about something you can do while you are here."

"Well, that would be good," Benny replied, "but what I really want to do is to get back on the road again, headed home. Maybe we should have stayed in England with our grandparents."

Tom suggested they let Jacob get back to his work. "Let's go see what John is doing." Jacob said he could go with them, and Benny was okay with that. They found John at the medical facility. He had finished with his appointments for the day.

Jacob greeted John, "I am back, and if you or Carol need anything, you can call me now. The prison gang may be monitoring our CBs, so we have to be aware of that. We will soon have a solution to this problem."

John greeted them. Benny hugged him and said, "You sure do remind me of Dad."

Jacob took note of that. "Say, Benny, how would you like to work with your uncle? We can get you a lab coat. The nurse will give you the file folders on each scheduled patient, and you will go to the waiting room and take the patient to the next examination room. There are three exam rooms, and you will keep them all full. It takes about 15 minutes for Dr. John to examine a patient. When a room becomes empty, you get another folder from the nurse and get the next patient's name. You go to the waiting room and call out his or her name. Then this routine starts all over again. How does that sound, Benny?"

"I can do that," Benny enthusiastically replied.

Dr. John told Benny he would be glad to have him as his 'assistant.' "We could start your training right now. We could examine your brother Tom first."

"Me!" Tom exclaimed, "In a doctor's office?"

"Yes," John replied. "Then Susie and then David."

"Okay," Benny cheerfully agreed.

Jacob smiled. "My work here is done. I'm heading for the command center. I'll be letting you all know more later about the use of your CBs. We nearly have a code ready to use."

The resident nurse took them back to the nurses' station. "You can see where Benny will be working." She took Benny to a closet that was full of lab coats. She got the smallest coat in the closet. It fit Benny pretty well. "You look good, Assistant Benny Robinson." Benny puffed up his shoulders and looked at Tom and Susie. The nurse pulled out a file folder and got an examination form. She wrote "Tom Robinson" across the top of it. She then asked Tom, Susie, and David to go to the waiting room. "Benny will get you when the doctor is ready to see you."

They left, and the nurse instructed, "Benny, follow me, and I will show you the exam rooms. There are numbers on each room. When you bring Tom into this room, you will ask him to sit on this exam chair." She handed Benny Tom's file folder. "Anyone with him can sit over there."

Benny laughed and repeated, "...anybody with him..."

"Put the file folder in the rack by the door when you leave. When the doctor comes in, he will grab Tom's folder."

Benny put the folder in the rack. The nurse took it down and handed it to Benny. She pointed at the name, "This patient's name is pronounced, Tom Rob-in-son."

Benny repeated, "Tom Rob-in-son. Got it."

"Go to the waiting room and call his name. Take him to exam room number one."

Benny dutifully held the file folder and called out, "Tom Robinson." Then, he exaggerated a searching look all around the room for someone he had never seen before. Tom slowly got up. Benny called out, "Come with me." He took him to exam room number one. Benny told him to sit on the exam bench, then he slyly said with a straight face, "Your imaginary girlfriend, Judy, can sit over there."

Benny quickly stepped back as Tom shook a fist at him. "The doctor will be in soon. You 'all' get comfortable." He put the file folder quickly into the holder, stepped out, and shut the door. He was smiling from ear to ear. Inside, Tom was also smiling.

The nurse handed Benny a new folder; she pointed at the name and pronounced, "Susie Rob-in-son."

Benny repeated, "Susie Rob-in-son. Got it."

Chapter 10

Susie, the Waitress

After their medical examinations, the Robinson family had visited with Uncle John and Aunt Carol for nearly an hour. The kids and David Billman were declared in good health by Dr. John. Tom knew that he needed to call Judy that evening and get her up-to-date on what was happening with them.

David declared, "I haven't had a complete health exam for a long time. I certainly didn't expect to get a health exam after the pulse. The people in this community are very fortunate to have this health service available. Dr. John's arrival makes this possible, and Assistant Benny makes it fun."

Benny liked all this attention, and he especially enjoyed being with his uncle. He knew they could get along without him, but he enjoyed doing it. He felt good this afternoon and was looking forward to working two or three hours each day.

After the exams, David Billman went back to his room. Tom told him they would get him later for their evening meal. The Robinson kids relaxed. Some of the tension from their Atlanta entrapment faded from their thoughts as they visited with their dad's brother. He talked a lot about their dad when they were young. The kids heard stories their dad had never told them.

At about 5:30 p.m., they decided to get David and eat. Tom asked John if he had ever had to pay at the restaurant?

"No, none of us from the hospital ever have."

Tom acknowledged, "None of us from Moline pay either, but a lot of people do pay with cash. These people must have gotten cash before the pulse." They found a table and sat down.

After waiting quite a long time, Rachel, herself, hurried to their table and apologized. "One of my girls didn't show up this evening, and I don't know if she ventured out of our protective community or what. I'm worried about her. She's always been a responsible girl. Do you want to order, or do you want to go through the buffet?"

Susie spoke up, "Let's go through the buffet. That will help Rachel." The others agreed.

Rachel looked at Susie and reflected, "You remind me a lot of my missing waitress. You seem very responsible."

"I am willing to try to fill in for this girl. I briefly filled in for a waitress once before the pulse."

"Oh, could you? That would be a lifesaver. Do you want to eat first?"

"No," Susie responded. "You probably need me now, and I'm not very hungry."

"Wonderful!" Rachel exclaimed. "Come with me."

The rest of them got up and headed for the buffet line. Benny assured everybody that he was hungry after all the work he had been doing. He caught Tom rolling his eyes. Benny smiled as he led the group down the line.

Tom saw Ezra, Jacob, and three other men going through the line in front of them. The visiting men had their plates piled high. Tom, David, and John knew the importance of these men. The warden and police chief would help find a solution to the prison gang.

Ezra's group got their food and went off to some nearby private room.

Rachel got Susie a waitress uniform and an order pad. She quickly briefed her on the menus and how to address the customers. Susie assured Rachel, "I will do my best and try to learn as I go. Why do you think your waitress might have gone out of your community?"

"She has a boyfriend who lives outside. We think a lot of him. She's confided in me that things are getting worse out there. He has been getting groceries from our store. I hope she didn't venture out there."

When the Robinsons and David finished their meal, they told Susie they were going back to the kids' room to monitor their ham radio. They would soon try calling Judy and Kathy. Tom told Susie that they would call their parents after she got off work.

John and Carol were going to go back to their room. John commented, "I wish I knew what Ezra's group has learned and what they are planning before we leave."

Tom agreed. "Jacob is supposed to keep us informed. I wish we knew his information before we contacted Judy and Kathy. We will have to be very careful what we say because the gang might be monitoring ham radio calls."

As John and Carol left, John told Benny, "I will see you tomorrow at 9 a.m."

Benny smiled, "I sure will be there, Uncle John."

Tom decided that it might be too early for Judy to be back from Moline. He thought they should wait an hour before they tried calling. Maybe she would call if she got back earlier. Tom had still not heard from Judy after they had waited for an hour. He was about to call her when Jacob came by. He reported that the meeting with the warden and police chief had gone well. "They both are very anxious to bring down this gang. They are going to do all they can to help us. The warden has files on the likely leaders of the gang. He will bring us this information tomorrow. The police chief still has contacts with many of his men. He has promised active support in removing this menace."

Tom replied, "I'm going to use the ham radio you gave us to call our friends in Moline."

Jacob cautioned, "Be very vague about revealing any information that the gang might be able to use in some way. We will get you a copy of our just-finished codebook.* Also, we may be able to get one to your people in Moline. The police commissioner has a friend in the US Military who he has invited to our meeting tomorrow. He tells us that he is interested in getting food for the military. The police commissioner thinks that the military might send a truck to

Moline to get a load of bread. They could also take our codebook to your friends there."

Tom exclaimed, "That is good news!"

*The codebook is located at the end of the book.

Chapter 11

Settling In

Tom and David were ready to talk if they could get someone to answer. If Judy was not back, Kathy probably would not respond. Tom called and identified who he was. He asked Kathy to reply and gave instructions on using the radio. To his surprise, Kathy answered.

Tom immediately began talking. "We're all okay down here, but I caution you that we may have somebody listening in on our call. We must take some precautions. Don't mention last names, names of towns, and names of projects; for example, Judy's project. We won't mention what her project is. By the way, has Judy returned from that unnamed town?" Tom again told her what button to push to talk.

Kathy nervously answered. "Judy is not back yet. Is David there with you, Tom?"

"Yes. David is here."

David answered, "Are you okay, and have you had a good day?"

"Yes," Kathy answered. "I've been here by myself, except for Bruce. He has been out there almost all day working."

David interrupted, "Don't say what he's doing. Remember, just like Tom was saying, we won't talk in specifics of any kind."

"Okay," Kathy replied. "I'm afraid to talk, so I will just say we are fine, and I am glad you are all okay."

Tom said, "Kathy, could you have Judy call when she gets back? Please explain to her our restrictions."

Kathy signed off, saying, "I will."

Judy called about an hour and a half later. Tom answered, "Judy, I want to ask you all about what you've been doing today. Maybe I can ask you all about that tomorrow or the next day. So, tonight I'll say, I hope you had a good day, and I'll wish you a good tomorrow."

"Oh well, Tom, you were always a little short on words, so what's new? Anyway, you would never believe what I am getting done; we were successful in our main project. Does that tell you anything?"

"Yes!" Tom returned. "I appreciate that message—it does tell something that I am glad to hear. Kathy told me that Bruce was busy all day. Now, for your ears only, we think we're making some progress on our problem here. However, we still have no idea when it will be solved. We will be calling you or Kathy. Signing off, Tom, David, and Benny."

At 8:30 p.m., Rachel sat down with Ezra for a cup of coffee. She motioned for Susie to come over to their table. When Susie approached, Ezra asked, "Who is this new waitress?"

"She is the fine young lady who rescued me tonight when my regular waitress didn't show up for work. Susie was formerly known as 'The Shooter.' Now she is known as 'My Best Waitress.' Susie, can you come back tomorrow at about five?"

"Yes," replied Susie, "as long as we are here, I will be glad to help. We're hoping to get back to the Moline area and get on our bicycles and start our trip home to Kansas."

"You kids are very brave and dedicated to your parents. It will be a dangerous trip," Rachel sighed with concern. "Oh, by the way,

I've been meaning to ask you if it bothered you to think about having shot that pick-up driver chasing you?"

"Yes, that does bother me, and I think about that some, but I don't know if I actually shot him. I know I shot the windshield, and he could not have seen where he was going. I caused the truck to wreck, whether or not I hit the driver. I guess I did help our truck to get here."

"Thank you for that," was Ezra's comment.

Rachel told Ezra about her missing waitress. She asked him if he would send someone tomorrow to check on the girl's boyfriend's family and see if they might know where the girl was. Rachel told Susie that even if they found her missing waitress, she wanted Susie to keep working as long as she was still in Atlanta.

Susie thanked her and left to find Tom and Benny. They were waiting on her to call their parents. Tom reminded the kids that they needed the call to be brief because of the difficulty of talking in specifics. He told Susie they had spoken briefly to Judy and Kathy.

Tom got his parents on their ham radio. He cautioned them immediately that there was a slight chance that some bad people might be listening to their conversation. "This call will be brief, and we won't mention any specific names or places. We've had a good day. We're safe, and we've made some progress on our problem here. We still don't know how long it will take to correct it. Are you in town tonight, and have you had a good day?"

Their dad answered, "We have had a good day. We're still staying in town. Mom and I want to tell you all about our activities and hear about yours, but maybe some other time."

"Yes, some other time," Tom replied.

Susie and Benny said, "Goodbye."

Tom thought that it was really difficult and frustrating talking without saying anything. "Now, I think it is time for you two working people to get to bed. It seems like I am the only one who can't get a job and get settled in here." Susie and Benny laughed at Tom's plight.

Chapter 12

Judy's Progress

The Robinsons were beginning to settle into a routine while they were forced to stay in Ezra's community, waiting for a time when it would be safe to leave and go back to the Moline area. Meanwhile, they knew little about Judy's activities back in Moline. Judy had been busy after Tom, David, Susie, and Benny had left for Ezra's place in Atlanta.

It was Judy's first day after Tom and her brother David had gone into Atlanta and gotten trapped there. She didn't have Jack today; he had been called back to Ezra's compound and had ridden with the generator truck. Today, Judy invited her mother to go with her to Moline and help her with the bakery. After loading the antique Ford pickup with sacks of flour and two cream cans filled with water, Judy and Emily went to Gus's place. This morning, Judy and Gus were planning to bake a large batch of bread. Gus was very excited; he had been talking to the city council members and other important individuals. They were optimistically hopeful because of the bakery and the natural gas-fired electric generator.

They got to the bakery, and Judy and Gus wanted to get the bread in the oven first. Then Gus and Judy crossed their fingers. Judy introduced her mother to Gus. She mentioned that her mother would probably come with her every day to help with the bakery. "Now, we need to get another batch of bread dough made and get it in the bread pans to rise for the next batch of bread."

Gus got the sacks of flour from the truck and dumped them into the gravity bin. He brought in the cream cans of water. Judy moved the small portable generator outside the back door and got it started. That reminded Gus that the natural gas-fired generator that Ezra sent yesterday might not be ready to use today because they had found bullet damage late yesterday.

Gus worried out loud, "The men working on it will be able to fix it, hopefully, by tomorrow. In anticipation of this, some of the council is checking on getting the city waterworks ready to bring back online. Our council members are hopeful that we can save this town yet. We know that people have already suffered, but things are not totally out of control. If we can get these things coming online quickly, hopefully, we can save most everyone in this town and the surrounding area."

As Gus talked, they worked on making their dough and getting it into bread pans. Judy showed her mother things she could do to help. Before they finished with the dough, Joe arrived in the bullet-ridden car that Ezra had sent him. He brought Sara to stay and help. He said he would be back for the council meeting.

Gus announced, "I hadn't gotten around to mentioning that meeting yet. The council and interested people want to have their meeting here at 10 a.m."

Judy thought the bread should be baked by then. "Hopefully, we can sample some freshly baked bread at the meeting." She asked Sara, "Do you have an old-style coffee maker large enough for that group? If they are like Gus, I don't think they will need to be hyped-up any, but the coffee would be nice with the fresh bread."

Sara told Judy, "I have the coffee maker and coffee at my house." Judy offered to take her to her house to get it. They were beginning to get a hint of the smell of bread baking. They finished getting the next batch of dough into the bread pans and put it on the shelves to rise and be ready to bake.

Judy called to Sara, "Sara, let's go get the coffee maker and coffee." When they got back, the bread had finished baking. They started taking the bread out of the oven. While they were doing this, Joe brought in a load of people. They commented on how good it smelled. One of them said it smelled like a bakery. The mayor, who also had an antique car, delivered people. Judy set up some card tables and chairs close to the booths. Sara had brought plates, utensils, coffee cups, butter, and some bottles of water from her house. She placed these items on the tables.

Judy cut two slices of bread for everyone. Sara poured coffee and handed out water.

Joe started the discussion. "The mayor and I organized this meeting. Judy, you and Gus have just done the first big step that is our first goal. Our hopes require a few more of these big steps to happen to save this town."

The mayor interrupted, saying, "Well, I guess the first step that happened was what you did for us, Joe. You got the gas wells operating, making natural gas available to the town so the oven could operate here at this bakery. Gus played a big role in getting that oven operating."

"Well, yes," Joe agreed. "But Judy is our 'hero of the day.' This fresh bread really tastes good. The council was hoping for your success, and you have done it. So, I think our first issue to discuss is what we will do with our bread. The last time we talked, this question of how much bread we need to keep here in Moline was still not decided."

Judy assured the group, "We can decide later. Currently, we can use all the bread we want. Tom told me last night that it is not safe to travel in or out of Atlanta. I got the idea that it may stay that way for several days. So, right now, I don't think we need to hold back any of our production for Atlanta. That will let us see what our demand is here."

"All right," the mayor declared. "We have lots of starving and stealing people. What proposals do we have?"

It was unanimous thinking that people could not pay for bread. The council knew that no bank accounts were available without computers. No one had paychecks. The only choice was to provide free bread to the starving people.

The mayor asked, "Can we do that at least for a while? This bread starts with the wheat that David Billman owns. Can he keep supplying this wheat?"

Judy's mother spoke up, "David has wheat stored in bins. I think the bank has a lien on it. David's trapped in Atlanta, but I think he wants to make it available. I'm sure he would like to get paid someday."

"What about the grinding costs?"

Judy added, "David has a full fuel tank and a man named Bruce who is volunteering his labor to grind it. My mother and I will volunteer our services, and I think Gus will too."

"Okay," the mayor concluded, "We will plan to notify the residents of a free bread give-away. The council will meet every day and will try to come up with a plan to compensate everyone involved."

Chapter 13

Moline Council Meets

The council decided to provide free bread for the townspeople based on donated supplies and labor. The mayor expressed a desire to explore ways to provide payment for all costs involved in providing bakery products.

The mayor and the council discussed other projects they hoped could be achieved. Electricity was close to being attainable, and the natural gas-fired electrical generator would be ready soon. Council members were already looking at the transmission lines fried by the pulse. The mayor stood. "We are checking the lines coming to the bakery first. These lines come past the police department on the way to the bakery. It will be nice to get power to the police station in the process."

Joe spoke up when the mayor mentioned the police. "Judy, I would like for you to meet Moline's police chief. He has one of his deputies with him today. In our long meeting last night, we decided to provide security for the bakery. These deputies are willing to work free of charge, just like you plan to do. For this purpose, Ezra had planned to provide his soldier, Jake, but Jake is gone now, so we need to step up. The chief has deputies ready to start now and will provide at least one officer day and night."

"Good," Judy exclaimed. "We have some extra keys, and if the council would like to meet here every day, they are welcome. I want to try my hand at making donuts and cinnamon rolls. I think Sara has gotten me all the ingredients I need. Long term, I need to do some scouting for ingredients. We may be able to get what we need out of Atlanta. In England, we often made scones with berries in them, but I don't have any ingredients for that yet."

The mayor asked the group if anyone had any objection to meeting at the bakery. There were no objections. The mayor thought donuts and cinnamon rolls sounded wonderful to him. The police chief wholeheartedly agreed with the mayor. He added as an afterthought that the council had talked about providing security for Sara's grocery mart. Thieves had already looted the store once.

With security, Sara felt that she could open her store for limited hours. "I will be glad to sell bread and bakery products to people who have cash or 'credits.'" Sara was the first to bring up the word "credits." The council had talked about "credits" in their long meeting the night before.

The mayor reflected on last night's meeting, "We talked about a plan to give payments to people who provide goods and services. Values for goods and services will be agreed upon and set by the council. We'll issue credits for the amounts of goods and services. The bank could maintain the records of everyone's accounts at the bank. The banker's wife has volunteered to be in charge of these records. All values and credits will be based on our previous money units. We'll continue to use cash to the extent that it's available. A big banking chain owns our Moline bank. The current manager, or should I say, the previous manager before the pulse, Bob Grenold, and his wife are here." The mayor went on, " They tell me that the bank contains an average amount of cash. Currently, it's all locked up in vaults, but if the electricity was on, we could open them.

"Bob and his wife, Ruth, are longtime residents of Moline. They've been suffering after the pulse, just like all of us. You realize most of us here are not suffering like the majority of the people. We are privileged because we know Sara and Joe. We have been able to get food and bottled water from her store. These items are about gone now. Nobody has had a shower since the pulse. All of us in here are equally grimy as the other 3,000 residents of Moline.

"Speaking of a shower, Glory Hallelujah, we may even have one in our sights if we can get that big government surplus generator of Ezra's running! The pulse hasn't harmed the water pipes. Some new power lines may need to be installed going to the pumps. We should be able to get the pumps working before long.

"Anyway, I was talking about our banker family and their feelings about the people of our town. We are in the same boat. We are all facing the results of this pulse. None of us can do anything about the suffering of most of these people, but maybe we can do something to rescue the people in this town and the area around it. It looks like we may have an opportunity to do something. We need to push the opportunity to get all the benefits we can. We already have an operating bakery. Praise the Lord! We have a lot of people who are volunteering to do what they can. So, getting back to our banker family, because of their compassion for the suffering people of our community, they are willing to stick their necks out to take some personal risks. The bank building and its assets belong to someone else. We don't know what has happened or will happen to these owners. The prospects are not good for them, but we're not thieves, and we should hope for the best for the bank owners. We all realize that we're responsible for doing what is best for this community. It certainly won't hurt to use the building. We'll take good care of it.

"Now, as far as the use of some of the bank's cash... We need to set aside money or credits to pay for the use of its cash. The bank owners may come back someday, and if they do, we need to have an account available to pay them. If we do this, maybe we can justify putting the bank's cash into circulation to help our community come back to life.

"The community will need to hire more and more people as it comes back. We should get the egg production facility going as quickly as possible. The same is true of the broiler operation located close to town. The feed mill will need to hire people. All of these people will need to have the hope of getting paid. We are trying to devise a plan that could work. It's kind of like trying to begin civilization all over again. We don't want it to be a Ponzi scheme. We want it to be fair, and we want it to work. Keep thinking, people, because I believe we will try this if we don't come up with a better plan."

Meanwhile, back in Atlanta, Benny convinced his Uncle John and Aunt Carol to go to the shooting range with him. He made arrangements with Ezra to let them try the "Baby Glocks." Benny was interested in trying this gun himself. He knew the nine-millimeter gun would have more stopping power than his 22-caliber Smith and Wesson.

Tom and Benny had talked to John and Carol about getting guns. Neither John nor Carol had ever owned a handgun. They both agreed with Benny that now, after this pulse, was the time to be owning handguns. They had experienced the craziness of this new world while they were still at the hospital, so it wasn't hard for Benny to convince them. They also knew that guns were available from Ezra.

Today, Ezra sent three new Glocks with them to the firing range. One was for Benny to try. Benny was proud of his experience at the shooting range. He felt good taking the lead in showing his Uncle John and Aunt Carol the target practice experience.

John and Carol were quite willing to let Benny show them how to shoot the handguns. After it was all over, John and Carol each owned one of the handguns.

Chapter 14

No-Way Bart

Gus left the meeting and went to the back room to check the oven. When he came back, he announced that there would be another batch of bread ready in about an hour.

The mayor reacted, "It's time to get out and notify the people and get this bread into their hands. Judy, may we use your truck? That would give us three vehicles. We have three megaphones at city hall."

Judy agreed and said, "Sara can drive David's antique truck."

"We'll drive the streets announcing that the residents can pick up free bread in one hour in front of the police station. Later, we can put up signs listing the time for bread distribution in the future."

Judy knew this would give them time to get this second batch of bread out of the oven and ready to go. There would be plenty of bread to cover today's needs. More people would come next time. Word of mouth would spread the message.

Judy told the council, "I wish we had wrapping paper to put around the bread to keep it clean. People will have to handle this with their dirty hands as they did in ancient times. It was still being done this way in certain parts of the world before the pulse. Right now, people will be so happy to have a loaf of bread and be able to break off a piece to eat."

The mayor advised, "We should send a police officer with each vehicle making the announcement. We should also have an officer with each vehicle at the bread give-away. We'll load bread in the backs of the old trucks and distribute it from the tailgates in three lines. Judy, will you be all right without security for the rest of the afternoon?"

"Sure," Judy replied.

Gus announced that he was leaving to check on the progress of the electric generator. He hoped to find time to examine some of the power lines.

When the council left, Judy and her mother were alone. Judy thought they should prepare another batch of dough for bread. They had their work set out for them, but they could do it without Gus by working together.

The city was divided into three areas to canvass. Two people in each vehicle took turns announcing and driving. Sometimes people would hear them coming and would come out to the road. As soon as they were clear about the message, they would often start walking toward the police station. Many of the houses didn't have people come out. In some cases, people inside may have heard the message.

Sara saw a couple sitting on their front porch. They listened to the message and finally understood. They screamed back that they couldn't walk that far, and that they needed water more than bread. Sara got out of the truck and took her bottle of water to them. The old couple quickly shared it. Sara told them she would bring some bread and water either today or tomorrow. The people were very thankful but could hardly get back into their house. Sara and the policeman hurried on.

Meanwhile, back at the bakery, Judy heard the front doorbell jingle. Judy and her mother turned from what they were doing to see who was there. There he was—"No-Way Bart." A scruffy-looking man stood beside him. No-Way smiled, "There you are Judy, 'my Judy.'"

Judy came back loudly, "I have nothing to do with you, Bart!"

"Oh, but Judy, we have history, so you 'all' owe me."

"I owe you nothing, Bart! You need to get lost! What on Earth are you doing around here?"

"Nice of you to ask, but you should know that we are connected. I've been keeping an eye on you ever since I came to that grocery mart that your relatives own. I watched them, and they led me to you and this bakery. Now, ain't that lucky for us, Judy?" Bart and his buddy had edged closer to Judy and her mother.

Judy instinctively felt for her pepper spray and realized that she and her mother had left their pepper spray behind. She kept backing up as they moved closer. She made a mental note never to let that happen again.

"What do you want, Bart?"

"Oh, I want in on everything. That punk of yours always held out on me. By the way, where is Punk? I haven't seen him in the last couple of days. Where is he when you need him?"

"He is around."

"I don't see him, Judy. I smell bread. Are you holding out on me?"

Judy's mother bravely tried to rescue the moment by saying, "Bart, we can serve you some bread; do you want butter on it?" Bart seemed tempted. She instructed, "Sit down over there at the table. Do you want coffee?"

Bart looked at his scruffy buddy. "See, Zeek, I told you that it would pay to keep an eye on these people the last couple of days." Zeek took a couple of steps toward the table.

Judy's mother took two cups of coffee, a loaf of warm bread, and some butter to them. She sliced two pieces of bread for each of them. Bart moved over, sat down, and pulled out a gun, placing it on the table. Zeek was already eating. Bart buttered a slice of bread and asked Judy, "Aren't you going to join us?"

"We have bread baking in progress, and we must take care of it." Bart and his buddy kept eating hungrily.

Judy sighed with relief when she heard a truck returning. Looking out the window, they saw Sara heading their way in the truck. The officer was driving. When No-Way and his partner saw them, they finished gulping down their coffee and grabbed the remaining portion of the loaf of bread. They were on their feet as the truck pulled around the back to load.

Judy yelled, "Leave a tip!"

Bart yelled back, "We will keep in touch!"

Judy looked at her mother. "I sure was glad to see Sara and the officer. Thank you, Mom, for defusing this situation with that dreadful man. We must stay armed after this."

Chapter 15

Free Bread

Judy confided to her mother that she was getting pretty scared when Bart was there. "I think he gets scarier every time we run into him. He acts like he may be psychotic and dangerous. I'm glad we are going to start having security."

Judy and her mother got busy helping load David's truck with bread for Sara to take to the giveaway site. Judy made a mental note to ask Ezra if he could get her some wrapping paper for her bread. The other two trucks soon returned and were ready to be loaded. The mayor was with one of the trucks. Judy told him about Bart and asked to have an officer remain at the bakery.

"You've got it for sure, Judy. Most of the council members are going to be at the free giveaway," the mayor commented. "We're going to talk to the people about holding things together. We'll tell them about what we are planning for Moline. I'll make sure you have security from now on. We need to activate more of our former policemen."

The three trucks left for the police station, where a large crowd was gathering. Joe and some of the council already had people lined up in three rows. As the three trucks with bread pulled up, Joe had them back up to the head of each line. The mayor got out and stood in the back of one of the trucks. A police officer was in the back of each truck, ready to hand out the bread.

A number of the council joined the mayor on the back of the truck. The mayor had a megaphone. "Attention, please! Citizens of Moline! The city council and I are very sorry and concerned about what this terrible solar pulse has done to our country! We are most concerned about what it is doing to our local people. We know that many people will starve and die in our country. We can't do anything about that, but we are trying to do something about our local situation. I have several messages of hope for our town. This free bread project is our first effort. We don't want people to starve or steal to get food. We are providing police security at the bakery and the grocery store. Anyone with cash can buy more bread at the bakery or grocery store.

"We have been able to restore natural gas service to the east side of Moline. Eventually, it will be available to the west side. The natural gas service will be free until you have jobs. We hope that jobs will gradually become available. You may come to city hall tomorrow to start inquiring about employment.

"You may have heard about our large natural gas electrical generator that we are trying to get started. We hope to bring back electric power eventually. It may take some time to get power back because the pulse fried many of the transmission lines. We'll try to get electrical power to priority places first. For example, we want to get the water plant operating as soon as possible. Can you imagine what that will mean to all of us? Again, we will make free water available for people who have no jobs. We hope that we can have sanitary water for drinking in about a week."

A cheer rose from the crowd. The mayor picked up a loaf of bread and waved it around. "We'll give out bread again tomorrow at this same time! Spread the word! Anyone caught trying to steal will be prosecuted. Eventually, we will have other food items besides bread. We will keep you informed of progress each day." He handed his loaf to the first man in line. The officers passed a loaf to each person waiting. There was some pushing and shoving, but two people handed the bread out rapidly at each truck. Some people broke off pieces with their dirty hands and started eating immediately.

Halfway through the bread giveaway, the electrical workers' foreman came running to the mayor. "The generator is running, and some of the linemen are stringing new lines to the police station and city hall. You'll never believe our luck! We have found some transformers not being used to replace the burned-out ones!"

"Good! Let me tell the people this encouraging news."

After all the people got bread, there was still some left. The mayor picked up the megaphone and announced that the electric generator was working. "We might have power in city hall tomorrow. We may have additional announcements then."

When Sara was handing out bread in her line, she recognized No-Way Bart. She thought he remembered her because he looked her in the eye and had a smirk on his face. Sara recalled that Judy had told her Tom Robinson did not like him very much. She also knew he had intimidated Judy into giving him bread earlier that day. She refused to hand him a loaf when he stepped up for his free bread. "You got your share from Judy earlier!" No-Way demanded that she give him another loaf. The policeman motioned for him and his scruffy partner to get out of the line. No-Way and his partner left angrily. When she headed back to the bakery, Sara planned to tell Judy that she had seen No-Way.

Judy and her mother were wrapping things up for the day. They planned to return extra early in the morning to run a batch of donuts and cinnamon rolls. Judy had been used to that routine while working for her aunt at her bakery in England. There was bread left over from today's giveaway. They had today's production, and there would be a batch baking in the oven to take out when they came early in the morning, so they should have plenty of bread for tomorrow. They loaded bread for Sara to sell at her store. She had fixed the break-in damage and was going to open every afternoon. A security guard was now watching Sara's store. Judy and Emily said goodbye to their security guard at the bakery.

R. Wesley Ibbetson

Chapter 16

20	26	13	20

19	22	26	23	10	6	26	9	7	22	9	8

*This title can be decoded by using the Code Book located at the end of this book (page 146), or you can cheat and look up the name of the chapter in the Table of Contents in the front of the book.

The Robinson kids woke up early. Susie insisted on their group hug. She reminded them, "We will get back on the road again, and we will eventually get back home." Susie and Benny seemed to be in a good mood. They reminded Tom that they were now working people, and they had to get up and get around. "We're not like you, Tom," Benny grinned. "We have important things to do." Tom rolled his eyes.

They got David, went to the restaurant to get food, and sat down. Ezra came by with a cup of coffee and sat down, commenting, "You are getting around pretty early."

Tom answered, "Yes, you know when you have jobs, you have got to get up and get going."

"Sure," Ezra replied. "Have you heard from Judy?"

"We called her last night, and we cautioned her that even our ham radios might be compromised. We never talked in specific terms, but she said her project had been successful. So, I believe she baked some bread."

"Good. I wish we were able to get some of it. I'll think about that. We're learning quite a bit about the prison gang. For one thing, we know where the gangs' headquarters is located. They are operating from the prison where they had been incarcerated. However, that presents a problem. The warden does not want us to destroy his prison, which would be the quickest way to eliminate them. We could use some of our shoulder-fired missiles and wipe them out. The warden is hopeful that the country can recover from this pulse. He wants the prison available if that happens. We promised him that we would hold off and find another way to get the job done. We don't have that solution yet."

Ezra hurriedly left, saying, "I'm scheduled to meet with the general and the soldiers for breakfast. Maybe we can figure out something."

The Robinsons spent a leisurely time eating. Rachel stopped and visited with them. Tom told her that they thought Judy had successfully baked bread yesterday.

Rachel sat down when that was mentioned. "That does sound good; I just wish there was a way to bring some of it here."

Tom agreed. "Ezra said the same thing, and he planned to try to figure out a way to get it here."

"Good," Rachel replied as she was right back up and off. "See you all later, especially you, Susie."

It was too early for Benny to go to work. They decided to head over to the medical facility with Benny. When they got there, John, Carol, and other staff members were there.

John greeted the kids. He confided to the kids that he felt a sense of obligation to Ezra. He revealed that he had people scheduled today from outside Ezra's community. "These must be people who know about this place and have been coming here already for some reason. One of them is injured, and the other one has health issues. I'm wondering how I could ever help people anywhere else like I can here. If Ezra can make this community safe from this prison gang, I think we will be safe here from anybody else. So, kids, I want you to know what I'm thinking. I'm sorry that I got you down here and delayed your journey home. The picture that we saw here in Atlanta looked so bleak. We didn't think that we could ever survive in the turmoil that would develop. Now, this is a totally different picture. It now appears that here is where we need to ride out this event. If things become safe here, you kids might even want to consider staying here yourselves." Before anyone could comment, an injured person arrived who needed attention.

Tom asked John if this was the scheduled injured person. John shook his head no, he didn't think so. The kids and David got out of John's way.

Jacob arrived and followed up, checking on the injured man. When he was satisfied that the patient was being taken care of, Jacob came to where David and the Robinsons were. He explained, "Our soldiers were out doing their thing this morning and found this man. A soldier recognized him and brought him in. Today is his lucky day."

Tom asked, "How are things going in the fight against the gang?"

"We are monitoring their conversations and have learned that they are raiding a hospital today. It sounds like they are mainly after drugs, but this could be a trap. There is no plan to interfere with these raiders. We need to find a way to capture the 'main gang.' We have been hearing encrypted language or code words such as 'Queen Bee' that indicate they may be talking about us and know we are listening. Our runners have also seen spray-painted symbols close to our boundaries that may be their way of marking our location.

"There is an idea on dealing with the prison gang, that we are working on, but not talking about yet. Our own encryption code has been completed. You kids will get a copy of the codebook. This code is something we quickly came up with. It's pretty simple. In time, the gang will decipher it, but we are hoping we can eliminate them before they do." Jacob hurried off.

Carol came up to Tom and the kids. "We would be pleased to have you kids stay here with us if things get safer."

Tom looked at David and replied, "We have other obligations to consider. That sounds like that could be a wise choice, but we are committed to getting back to our parents. We enjoy being around you and John, and I understand your desire to be able to use the training that you and John have to help people. I think we are okay if you decide to stay. We will let you get to work, and we will try to call David's wife on our ham radio." Susie hugged Carol, and they waved goodbye.

David acknowledged that he would be happy to talk to Kathy. She didn't hesitate to answer this morning. David talked to her, then Tom, using encrypted words, asked her if Judy was still making progress. "Oh yes, I think so; she and her mother had so much to talk about last night. They left extremely early this morning. Bruce is here today, working on his project," she said, trying to be discreet.

Tom replied, "Kathy, we will call his project 'skinning the squirrel.' We are sending a runner to you because we have a need here for 'tanning the squirrel' and for some 'bird droppings.'" He laughed after that and said, "I'll explain that later. A copy of our codebook is coming to you."

Tom thought Kathy's information sounded good, "We are okay, and our hopeful message is that we have the beginnings of a plan to solve our problem here in Atlanta. Have a good day."

Chapter 17

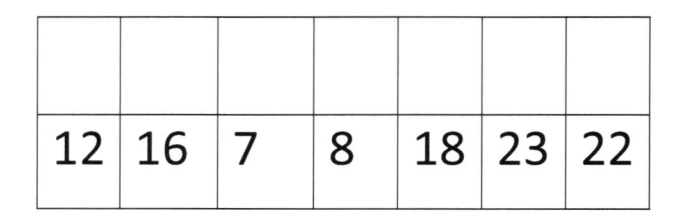

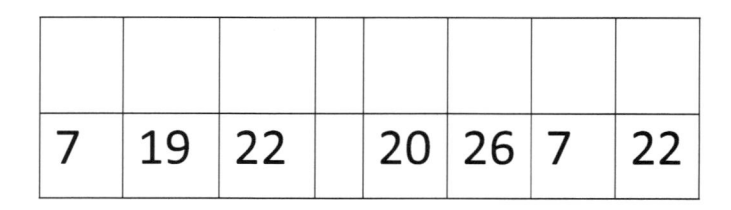

12	16	7	8	18	23	22

7	19	22		20	26	7	22

    The Robinson kids and David Billman were up early and made their way inside Ezra's compound to his hidden restaurant. Outside this concealed area of comfort and safety was the huge city of Atlanta. An entirely different kind of day was facing this unfortunate mass of people. Most of these people were not looking forward to a well-stocked buffet line like the Robinson kids were. Nearly all of these Atlanta citizens had been caught unprepared by the unannounced solar pulse. These people were waking up to the spectacle of starvation and danger from a crazy world.

The Robinsons could see that the restaurant had just opened. A few people were already there ahead of Tom and his siblings. Susie saw two kids sitting over to one side. These kids had not gotten in line as the café opened. Susie couldn't help but notice this boy and girl looked and acted a little different from the other customers. The boy was about Benny's age and had dirt on his face. The girl's hair looked like it hadn't been washed or combed for a while. Susie and Benny stopped to stare at them. Tom and David continued walking.

Benny impulsively stepped toward the two kids and pointed to the customers walking in to eat. He said to them, "The café has opened. You can go on in."

The two kids stood up and hesitated. The girl answered, "Oh no, we are just waiting for school to start. It will start in about an hour."

Benny exclaimed, "That's a long time. Have you already eaten?" The boy looked at his sister, and she shook her head, no. Benny continued, "Well, aren't you hungry?" The boy nodded his head that he was.

The girl sat down. "No, we don't have any money for that." Susie and Benny were shocked into silence. They had not expected to see anyone from the outside. They immediately felt bad for these kids who were about their age. Susie finally looked at Benny, and he looked at her. Benny quickly told Susie that he had some cash with him.

"Good!" Susie exclaimed, "Let's treat today."

"Okay," Benny agreed as he stepped over closer to the two and explained that he and Susie had extra cash and would like to buy their breakfast.

The boy jumped up excitedly, but the girl hesitated, "Oh no, we can't let you do that. Cash is too precious these days. Our folks gave us just enough to buy groceries here tonight before we come home."

Susie spoke up again, "We have plenty of cash; we are fortunate. We knew the pulse was coming, and our parents made sure that we had plenty. We also aren't having to pay for our food here at this place, so come on, we'll get you something to eat."

Benny put his hand on the boy's shoulder, "Come on." The boy moved out with Benny, and the girl also started walking.

The girl looked at Susie, "I don't know how to thank you for this."

Susie quickly responded, "Don't worry about it. It's okay."

Tom came back to see why the kids weren't coming. When he was satisfied that they were in line, he went back to join David. Susie led the kids to the cash register, and Rachel was working there. Rachel greeted the Robinson kids. Susie told Rachel that they wanted to pay for their two new friends.

Rachel shook her head, "Oh no, if these two are with you, they won't have to pay." Susie and Benny both thanked her. "I will see you this evening, Susie." The two outsider kids were in awe at the response from Rachel.

"Wow, wow!" was all the little boy could say.

Benny asked him, "What is your name?"

"Mikey!" They each got a big plate and started down the line. "Wow, wow!" Mikey exclaimed again. "Where did they get all these eggs to scramble for this large tray? The stores have been empty for days."

"Yes, Mikey, you're right!" Barbie agreed with her brother but looked at Susie and Benny as she continued to talk. "There's no food in the stores now. Our family is not starving because we are allowed to buy groceries from your 'inside the gate' store. We got enough money to buy groceries because your nurse told our mother to go to the bank and get as much cash as she could. The nurse insisted that our parents get that cash. It was the day before the pulse. The nurse did not tell us that the pulse was coming, but she had to have known. She did tell us about the grocery store here inside the gate that would allow us to buy food. We only have enough money to buy food for one month if we're careful. Look at all the food in this cafe!"

"Fill your plates full!" Benny encouraged. "I always do!" They got their food and went to a table close to Tom and David. Susie introduced the kids to them. Susie asked the girl what her name was.

"I'm Barbie." After learning that the Robinson kids and David were outsiders, Barbie and Mikey were a little more relaxed. Mikey devoured his food like he had not eaten for a long time, and Barbie lost interest in talking for a while as she concentrated on the wonderful food on her plate.

Ezra, Jacob, and some other men came by and spoke to Tom and the group. Ezra commented as he hurriedly greeted them, "Today, Tom, we have the police chief and prison warden bringing a special guest from the nearby National Guard and military facility who wants to talk to us. I just wanted to tell you this so that you would know that we may be making progress on our problem that is keeping you here."

"Thank you," Tom replied. "We appreciate that bit of information."

"We hope it will be helpful." Ezra and the other men hurried off to a private room.

Barbie asked, "Was that the Ezra who is the top guy of this inside place? Why did he stop and talk to you? What makes you so important?"

"Maybe, " Susie responded, "It's because we brought in a truckload of potential food."

David added, "We are also grinding wheat into flour. We may get a bakery going! Doesn't that sound exciting?"

"Ooooh," Barbie responded, "That would make you very important to the people here. They are managing to keep plenty of food around so far. Our parents are glad for Mikey and me to come here and go to school. On top of that, we can buy groceries on our way home. Speaking of school, it is time for Mikey and me to be going to class."

"We'll walk you there," Susie responded.

On their way to the school, Barbie mentioned she noticed that both Susie and Benny were carrying handguns. She observed, "A lot of the people in this place carry guns."

When they got to the school, a lady met the group at the door and told them to come in. Susie and Benny both replied, "No, we are just walking our new friends to class."

"Well, why aren't you coming to school?"

Susie responded, "We are just visiting this community and will not be here long."

"You can still attend while you are here. We are just getting our classes started. What grades are you in?"

Benny interrupted, "I would have to leave at 9 a.m. 'cuz I have a job to go to."

"You can leave any time you need to. We have classes for all ages, and you are welcome to come."

Tom and David had followed the kids. Tom told Susie and Benny that it was okay with him if they wanted to enroll in school.

Chapter 18

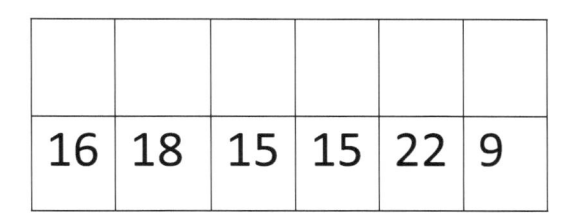

16	18	15	15	22	9

23	12	20		11	26	24	16

At 9:00 a.m., Benny slipped out of class. When he enrolled in her class, he had informed the teacher that he would need to leave at that time. Benny had also told Mikey that he would meet him after class. Benny enjoyed his work. He liked being around Uncle John. Today after work, Benny quickly left to find his new friends. Susie got out of class at the same time as their new outsider friends, Mikey and Barbie. They were on their way to the compound's grocery store when Benny found them. The outsider kids had a list from their parents, which they quickly filled. Barbie whispered to Susie, "We

usually wait until after dark to go home with our sacks of groceries. That way, no one can see our food and try to steal it."

Benny volunteered, "I can go with you. I have a gun on my hip and one hidden in my boot. I should be able to wave my gun at any robbers and scare them away."

"Oh, Benny," Susie laughed, "You're not a bodyguard!"

Benny defended his reputation, "I've been going to the shooting range every day since we got here, and I'm getting good at hitting the target."

"I know, Benny!" Susie continued. "You should ask Tom before you'd go out where it might not be safe."

Benny asked Barbie, "How far do you live from here?"

"It's just two blocks."

"Oh, well," Benny replied, "That's close and should be safe. I'll be back in a few minutes, Susie. I'll meet you in our room."

Susie threw up her hands and left. Benny followed the two kids to the closest outside gate, where they stopped to be checked out. The kids rolled up their sleeves, and the gatekeeper appeared to scan their arms.

Benny asked, "Do you have a bar code on your arm?"

"Yes," the kids replied. "It's just a temporary bar code. Mom and Dad were surprised that the insiders had working computers after the pulse. They have a lot of people coming in for things like groceries. The guards scan everybody in and out. The insiders keep a pretty close watch at the gate to their walled-in area. Since we live close to the compound, we are fairly safe. However, most of Atlanta has become very unsafe. We usually don't worry much unless it is the day we get groceries. Our parents want us to wait until dark to carry them out. It's hard for our dad to get away to come with us because he needs to stay close to our mother, who is injured."

Benny asked, "What happened to her?"

"She got into a car accident when the pulse happened." She continued, "Our parents won't care that we are coming in the daylight if you are coming with us."

The gatekeeper looked at Benny thoughtfully, "You probably don't have a bar code, do you? Are you one of the Moline kids?"

"Yes," replied Benny. "We are just staying here a few days."

"Okay," the gatekeeper returned. "Are you planning to be out long?"

"No," Benny replied. "I am just going two blocks with my new friends to their house. They don't have a gun, and their parents are concerned about their safety while carrying groceries. I will be right back in just a few minutes."

"Okay," the gatekeeper replied. "I think it would be best if you came right back."

The kids casually talked as they walked along. Benny relaxed, "I would like to go to school with you again in the morning for a while. I'll meet you at the restaurant for breakfast."

They passed the first block, and Mikey pointed, "That's our house at the end of this next block."

As they passed the alley, they heard a low growl. The kids turned their heads at once and looked toward the sound. The kids were petrified to see three large, hungry-looking dogs crouching there, teeth bared and growling. The dogs were about 50 feet away. The lead dog, the biggest in the pack, took a few steps toward them. The kids instinctively retreated a few quick steps in the direction of Mikey and Barbie's house. The dogs sensed the kids' fear. The lead dog jumped out front on the run.

Benny automatically grabbed his gun from its holster and pointed it at the charging dog. The dog had closed half the distance between them when Benny fired and hit it in its shoulder. The dog flinched but kept coming. Benny fired again, this time hitting the big animal in its head. It hit the ground, sliding close to where the kids all were standing, petrified. The second big dog had been right behind the first. Benny quickly aimed for its head. Firing, he hit it in the jaw. It continued to charge forward. Benny's second shot got it between the eyes. The dog dropped right at his feet. Before it hit the ground, he fired at the last dog, hitting it and causing it to stop right in front of them. The dog howled, turned, and limped back down the alley.

Mikey and Barbie had come out of their trance and bolted toward their home. As that third dog continued to run away down the alley, Benny thought about shooting him. His hands were shaking so much he couldn't shoot, and the dog was no longer a threat. Standing there trembling, Benny was in no hurry to follow the kids who had run to their house. Benny was going to stand there until he could stop shaking. Before Benny could decide to move, one of Ezra's runners ran up with his weapon out, ready for action. Benny started relaxing immediately.

The runner stood there looking at the two dead dogs and then looked at Benny. He commented, "It looks like you have this situation taken care of." Benny again felt shaky and emotional. He was close to tears. When Mikey, Barbie, and their dad arrived, Benny got control of his emotions. Benny pointed toward the approaching family. He was relaxed enough now to speak to the runner. "I was walking these two kids home because they were afraid to come home in the daylight with groceries. It turned out that it wasn't people that they needed to fear. I never thought about dogs becoming killers. I realize now that I'm not ready to be protecting anyone. This situation scared me to death!"

Mikey's family was listening to Benny talk. Barbie hugged Benny, and he noticed that she was trembling, too. She introduced Benny to her father. Barbie's dad shook hands with Benny and thanked him for being there and saving his kids. Then, he asked if he could see Benny's gun. Benny gave it to him.

He commented that it was still warm. "We do not own a single gun. Now we live in a world where it is not safe without one."

Benny volunteered, "We can get you guns. Ezra has lots of them."

Mikey's dad shrugged. "We are like everyone after the pulse. We have no money. We only have enough cash for food for a month. The nurse who has been coming to treat my wife urged us to get extra cash. There is no food anywhere else now. We are dependent on the groceries from this store. I am afraid to let my kids walk the two blocks to go to school and get groceries."

"We will get you guns. No problem!" Benny assured him.

"But we can't pay for them."

"I don't think that will be a problem." Benny thought that was what Tom would say. "My big brother, Tom, has gotten guns for people before." Then, Benny remembered he had two guns. Reaching in his boot, he pulled out his boot gun and handed it to Mikey's dad, saying, "This one is not so hot. It is my extra gun. You can have it, and it will solve your problem for now. Bring it with you tomorrow if you walk your kids to school."

"I will take it for now." He smiled as he held up Benny's .22 Smith and Wesson.

Benny looked at Mikey and Barbie, "Tomorrow! Breakfast!" They waved at him as he left with Ezra's runner.

Chapter 19

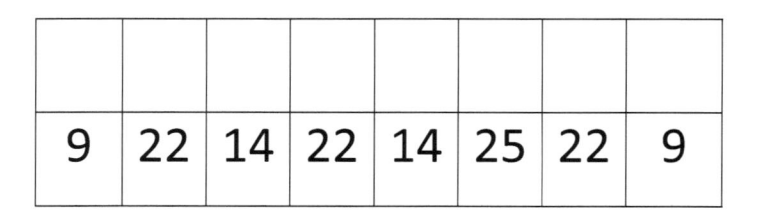

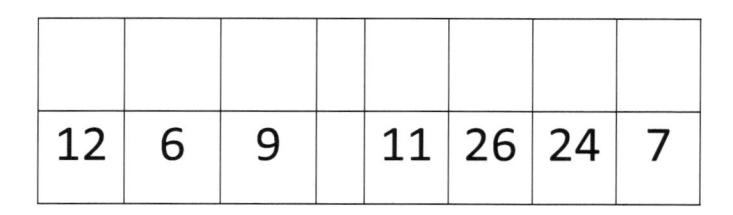

9	22	14	22	14	25	22	9

12	6	9	11	26	24	7

    Tom and Susie were waiting at the gate when Benny and the runner returned. Susie had told Tom that Benny was going out, which caused Tom great concern. When they went to the gate to check on Benny, they heard the shooting. The gate guard sent out a runner immediately, and he told Tom and Susie to wait there.

When Benny and the runner came up to the gate, Susie screamed, "Are you okay, Benny?"

Benny looked at her sheepishly. "I'm okay, Susie. I'm sorry I went off by myself like that, but if I hadn't, Mikey and Barbie would probably be dead right now."

Tom could see that Benny was shook up. He asked Benny, "So, you were involved in the shooting that we heard?" Benny nodded his head that he was. Tom put his arm around Benny. "Let's go back to our room and sit down and talk about it."

The kids got to their room, and Susie got after Benny immediately. "Benny, you forgot about our pact! You should never have gone out there without Tom and me. We always need to be together so we can protect each other."

"I know," Benny whimpered. "I totally forgot; I didn't stop to think. I didn't know that there could be packs of dogs out there that would attack people. What has gone wrong with them? They must have been someone's pets at one time."

Tom joined the conversation, "So, that is what happened? A pack of dogs attacked you, and you shot at them?"

"Yes," Benny stammered. "There were three of them, and they charged us. I killed two of them and wounded the third."

"The gate guard counted five shots," Tom recalled.

"Yes, I guess that would be right. I was so scared! I have never faced anything like that, and I am still shaking. I hit the lead dog in the shoulder with my first shot. It didn't slow him down much, so I hit him in the head with my second shot. It dropped him. The second dog—I hit him in his jaw, but he kept coming. My next shot got him between the eyes. That's what you have to do to stop them—at least if you have a .22 caliber gun like mine. Maybe I need to get a bigger caliber gun with more stopping power."

Tom broke in, "We'll look into that, Benny. I think you've gained some experience that may be helpful to all of us. Now, Benny, we have got to think as a team. We may have to face many dangers like this before we get home. So, we have to remember our pact to stay together to help keep us all safe. However, it looks like you saved these two kids' lives today, so that was a good thing. We never know what may happen, but we need to plan to try to anticipate the danger and be as safe as we can."

David knocked on the door and stepped in. He asked how Benny was. Tom answered, "Benny has been explaining what happened and is beginning to relax some. We were talking about why these pet dogs would start attacking people."

David announced that he had talked to Jacob about Benny's experience. "Jacob told me that people soon ran out of dog food after the pulse. The owners turned their pets loose to fend for themselves. Dogs tend to gather in packs in situations like this. For the most part, the only thing they find to eat is dead people."

"Oh, no!" Susie exclaimed. "Surely not!"

"I'm afraid it is," David continued, "and the next leap from there is to attack live people just like starving wolves do. We'll have to be alert to watch for these starving animals."

"I agree," Tom joined in. "We must remember this danger! We're going to look into getting Benny a gun with more stopping power."

"Jacob also told me that the prison gang may not have started monitoring the ham radios yet, but we need to start talking in code when we use them."

Tom thought about calling Judy. "Let's call and see how their day went, and then the kids and I will call our parents. We can start giving them some of our code words if we can do that without giving away too much information."

Susie had gone off to work for Rachel. Tom decided to wait until she got back before calling home.

When Tom called Judy, Kathy answered. Tom handed the mic to David, and he told her that they thought they could have a regular conversation this time, but they would have to start using code words after this. Kathy exclaimed, "Oh, okay. Judy is back and will be available in a few minutes."

"Ezra is visiting with some military men today. Military involvement has to be a good development. We have no idea how functional the military is after the pulse, but we may find out."

"Good," Kathy responded. "Here is Judy, and she's not a happy camper."

Tom spoke up, "Judy, what's wrong? What's happened today?"

"You'd never believe what happened today. That No-Way Bart showed up at the bakery when Mom and I were there by ourselves. He had a sleazy-looking guy with him. No-Way was acting threatening and a little crazy. Mother got them some bread and butter and some coffee. This kind of saved the day, I think. When Sara arrived with a police officer, No-Way and his sidekick took off. On a different topic, Kathy told me we can talk freely?"

"Yes," Tom responded.

"We baked bread again today and gave it out to the people of Moline. The city council meets here every day, and we discuss all kinds of plans. The council is looking forward to tomorrow's meeting because there will be cinnamon rolls and donuts."

"Wonderful!" Tom yelled. "I wish you could send some of that good stuff to us tomorrow. We hope things can develop here that will speed up our return, but we're not sure of that yet. Judy, what are you going to do to stay safe in Moline?"

"Mother and I are going to be armed in the future. The city council will provide a police officer for the bakery day and night. They said they would do this only if there were donuts involved. No, I'm just kidding. There is going to be day and night security."

"Good," Tom responded. "I won't tell you what Benny did today. He took a risk that he should never have taken. It turned out okay. He is alive, and two others are also alive because of him. We got after him for not including Susie and me in his risky decision to help his friends, but we are proud of what he did. There is a lesson here for all of us, Judy. Always have a weapon with you."

"You can fill me in on his adventure later. Say, I just remembered that I called Ezra and asked him if he could find a place that could supply a suitable kind of paper that I can use to wrap my bread."

"I will ask him if he has had a chance to look into that for you. You stay safe. We miss you! Goodbye."

Tom thought about Judy's request. "Let's go get Susie tonight, Benny, when she gets off work. Ezra might be there at that time for coffee. If we can catch him, maybe we can find out more about why the military is interested in this prison gang. We could also ask him about getting wrapping paper for Judy's bread and a copy of the Codebook that he and his runners are using."

Chapter 20

7	22	9	9	12	9	18	8	7

24	12	13	13	22	24	7	18	12	13

 Tom and Benny stopped by David's room and got him to go with them to the restaurant. They knew that David would be interested in what Ezra might have to say if they found him. It was about time for Susie to get off work. They didn't see Ezra when they came in. It was still a busy place. They got a table, and Susie came by and took their orders. Tom and David ordered coffee, and Benny ordered a Pepsi. When she brought the drinks to their table, she winked at Benny and said, "Here is your coffee." Benny smiled; he was glad that Susie had forgiven him and was trying to cheer him up.

Susie mentioned, "Rachel has her regular waitress back, but she wants me to continue working this same schedule."

Tom asked, "What happened to her regular waitress?"

"Ezra sent runners out to her boyfriend's home, and she was there. Her boyfriend was afraid to come out of his house. He had been robbed and roughed up by some evil neighbors. They were stealing the groceries he was bringing from here. The waitress went to check on him, and the hooligans chased her into the boy's house. She was afraid to come out because the thieves were watching. Ezra's runners took care of that little gang."

At that moment, Ezra and Jacob walked in. They headed over to the Robinsons' table. Ezra and Jacob ordered coffee. Ezra announced that he had several things to tell them. "First of all, I have found the bread wrapping paper that Judy wants. I am getting the person who will supply this paper with the things he needs to personalize it. He can design and color it to fit any wording Judy wants. I've given him a ham radio, so Judy needs to call him and tell him and place her order. We'll try to get a good supply of this bread wrapping paper so you can take it to Judy when you head back.

"We're making progress on solving the prison gang problem. I think the military is going to be our solution. It seems that America's military had prepared to some extent for this pulse event. So, they are partially functioning now. The military has more capabilities than any of us. Some of their vehicles were hardened to withstand this pulse. They have their own communications equipment that is still functioning.

"Our government is also functioning to a limited extent. There is some communication between countries. The military people who came today told us there is a terrorist connection with the prison gang. It seems that our southern border guards caught a group of suspected terrorists trying to sneak across the border. The government incarcerated that group here in Atlanta. There were other groups caught in California and Texas. They were all put in this Atlanta prison.

"Anyway, these military representatives say they will take care of this prison gang for us. This is excellent news. They didn't say how or when, but I will sleep well tonight. We had noticed that there was always one suspected terrorist in every car we blew up. The warden also told us he thought the leaders of this gang were members of these suspected terrorist groups. The military had previously contacted the warden about this issue, so he invited them to come to a meeting here. The military says the US government is worried about this terrorist gang. The government believes that this gang may try to take advantage of us while we are weak from this pulse.

"Anyway, Tom and David, there may be an end in sight for this prison gang. That means that you may be free to go home soon."

Susie and Benny cheered. Then Susie stopped cheering because she didn't want to offend Ezra. "We have really enjoyed your place, Ezra."

"I know you have, Susie, and we have wanted to make it pleasant for you. In fact, we would be glad for you to stay. We are going to make an offer to John and Carol to stay.

"On another topic, the military is very interested in helping with innovative food production. They even suggested they could provide transportation for food items coming from the Moline area. The military has offered to provide security, but, of course, they want a share of the food. We will have to see how the details can be worked out."

Tom responded, "These developments sound like a good thing, but they probably won't affect my sister and brother and me because we are committed to getting back home. It is tempting to stay here in the comfort and security of your community, Ezra. You have treated us so well and made us feel welcome. I think Susie and

Benny will agree with me that we need to move on when it becomes safe."

"I thought that would be your decision," Ezra commented. When Susie got off work, they headed to their room to call their parents.

On the way, David commented, "That news about the military being interested in our food projects in the Moline area could mean a lot to the people living there. They could bring a lot of safety and security to us. It could mean that civilization was closer to coming back.

"Tom, Susie, and Benny, you might want to consider staying with us in the Moline area. You could get in on the ground floor in these emerging industries and be much safer than on the road. Another positive is, you wouldn't starve."

"You are probably right," Tom agreed. "It is something for us to think about."

As an afterthought, David mentioned he thought his niece, Judy, would like to see them stay as well.

Benny quickly responded that they were about to call their parents to tell them they would soon get back on the road heading their direction. They said goodbye to David when they came to his room.

Their parents were very happy to hear their kids might soon be free to leave Atlanta safely. Their mom sincerely stated, "Kids, I hope this is the last time that you will ever be in that giant starving city."

Tom responded, "We have been encouraged to stay in the Moline area and become a part of the food-producing enterprises that could send some food into Atlanta."

Martha, their mom, quickly responded, "You can be involved in food production here. We are trying to start some food production here to help alleviate starvation. Being far from any large population center should make us a much safer place to live."

Susie and Benny both agreed. Susie spoke optimistically. "We may know as early as tomorrow if it is safe to leave here."

"Good! We have been hoping that you would get out of there soon," their dad replied. "Be sure to let us know as soon you know. Say, we talked to your grandparents and told them about you getting trapped in Atlanta. Maybe you could also call them when you get out of there."

"We will do that," Tom replied. "We miss you, and we'll talk to you later. Goodbye."

Chapter 21

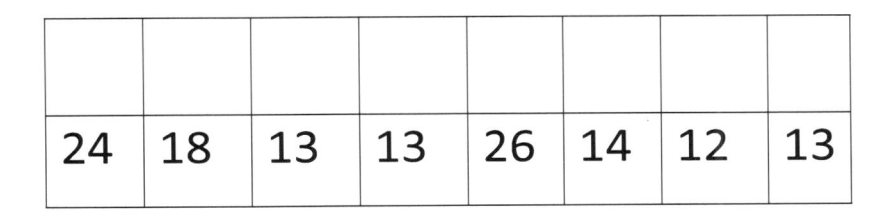

24	18	13	13	26	14	12	13

9	12	15	15	8

Judy and her mother got to the bakery early. Judy shuddered when she thought about the encounter with No-Way Bart yesterday. Sara and Joe promised them they would acquire handguns for them today. Judy knew they probably should be staying at the bakery instead of driving seven miles from her brother's farm every day.

The security guard was there and let them in. "I've been guarding these donuts and cinnamon rolls all night. I'm sure you know how important these are to policemen," he chuckled. "By the way, I could've put them in the oven, and you wouldn't have had to come over so early. Just tell me how to set the oven, and I can do that for you."

Judy cheerfully answered him, "Great! I sure will be glad to do that."

Sara and Joe arrived at the bakery at 9 a.m. Sara announced, "We have been to the farm store, and we got both of you a handgun. We got you the baby Glocks with holsters. Beware, No-Way Bart! Our bakery girls are armed. The farm store manager was very excited about everything going on here in Moline."

Joe smiled eagerly and declared, "I need to test these cinnamon rolls to make sure they are okay for the council members' meeting later this morning. Mmmm, these will do, but I better take a few donuts with me when I check the gas wells this morning. I'll be back for today's meeting."

Judy smiled as Joe made over her treats. She and her mother were also enjoying them.

Emily said, "My sister in England taught you well, Judy."

Judy acknowledged that her aunt was "good at what she does." "I would like to make some of the other British treats, but I don't have the ingredients. Our main focus needs to be on making bread."

Joe announced before he left that the bakery might get water today. "Judy, you may not have to bring over water from your brother's farm when you come tomorrow. We also may have electrical power for you in the morning."

Judy and her mom cheered. Joe hurried out with his treats. About 30 minutes later, Judy and her mother heard the front doorbell jingle. Two men walked in. One of them said, "Customers." Judy stepped into the front and saw No-Way Bart and his sidekick.

She hesitated and then blurted, "You forgot to leave a tip yesterday."

Bart spoke up, saying, "Good morning to you, too! I'm very glad to see you." The two of them found a table and sat down.

Judy stepped farther into the room, "Do you have cash? We only serve paying customers here."

"Oh, yes, we do have cash," No-Way smugly replied.

"Where did you get your cash, Bart?"

"Well, well, my Judy, don't you know that your friend is a man of means? Say, where did you get that sidearm? I need to get me one of those."

"You are not my friend, Bart! I got the sidearm for people like you who don't leave tips."

"Oh my, you are unfriendly! What about service? I'm hungry, and I need coffee."

The fully uniformed security officer stepped out of the backroom and asked Judy if she needed some help.

Judy smiled triumphantly and announced, "Yes, would you get an order pad and take these gentlemen's orders?" She emphasized the word "gentlemen." The officer smiled and said he would be happy to take their orders. No-Way Bart and his friend remained silent. They both ordered two donuts and a cinnamon roll to go with their coffee. Judy and Emily had discussed how they would price their bakery products. They also had talked to the city council about their pricing. Bart and his buddy ate in silence. Emily gave them a refill on their coffee.

Judy came in and presented them with their ticket. Bart got out his billfold and paid and left her a pretty good tip. Another man and woman walked in as Bart and his friend got up to leave. No-Way looked at Judy to see what she might say as they departed.

Judy thought for a moment and looked at him, "No-Way, this experience that you and I have just had may be the beginning of a return to the life that we all lost when the pulse hit. You were a customer who paid for a service that we feared was gone forever. Aside from our personal history differences, I feel that this happening is significant to the recovery of a functioning society."

Bart shrugged his shoulders and replied, "I think I understand what you are saying, and it would be nice to have things back the way they used to be." He paused and turned around. "Those sweet treats were pretty good." He dropped his gaze and walked out.

Judy turned and welcomed the couple that had walked in. The lady commented, "It's wonderful to walk in and smell the cinnamon rolls. After all this time without any hope of any future, your talk of recovery is refreshing. The smell of hot coffee is also rewarding."

"Sit down. Would you like cinnamon rolls or donuts or both? You may stick around if you wish. The city council will soon be meeting. They will be discussing more optimistic plans for the future."

Meanwhile, at Ezra's compound in Atlanta, there was optimism about the military taking care of the prison gang. The Robinson kids had met for breakfast with their new friends Mikey and Barbie from "outside the gate." Their dad had walked them safely to the gate this morning. He carried the gun that Benny had given him.

The outside kids brought troubling news to the Robinsons this morning. They had seen large crowds outside. The crowds had been mumbling about knowing that there was food inside the gate. When Mikey and Barbie entered the compound this morning, several men drove through the gate in a military Jeep.

Chapter 22

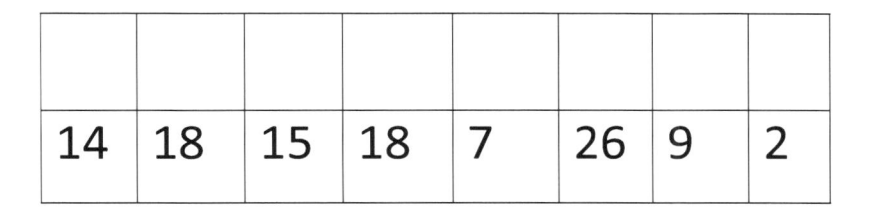

14	18	15	18	7	26	9	2

9	22	8	24	6	22	

Tom and the kids saw the four military men come into the restaurant. They were dressed in their full military uniforms and were easy to spot. Ezra and some of his men met them and escorted them to a private room.

Rachel spotted the Robinsons and asked Susie if she would like to help her for a while. Susie agreed that she would be glad to help. Rachel added, "Good, I wasn't expecting this group of military men. Come with me. Get your uniform and a pad. Go to room four and take their orders."

Tom thought Susie would learn how the military planned to deal with the prison gang. As Susie started to leave with Rachel, Tom told her to keep her ears open. Susie indicated that she would, then hurried to get her uniform. She popped over to room four as the men were getting seated. She told them she would take their orders when they were ready.

Most of them wanted coffee. Ezra answered for them, "Take our orders for drinks, and then we will go through the buffet line." Ezra added, "When you bring our coffee, bring a pot as well." Susie quickly returned with a cart and started passing around their drinks. An important-looking military man was not wasting any time. When Susie returned, he explained that the government had worked out a plan to catch these suspected terrorists. "Our government thinks they know what this group was planning to do. The government feels that these terrorists may still try to carry out their plan. The government has decided to put this gang back into prison."

Ezra commented, "This plays into our hands because it will help us to solve our prison gang problem."

Susie listened as she distributed the drinks. Then, she stood by with the coffee pot. It wasn't long until some needed refills.

Ezra asked, "How do you plan for this to work out?"

"All we need from you is for your scouts to watch the prison gangs' habits. Let us know when all of the gang is back at their headquarters in the prison. We will take it from there. We will surround the prison and starve them out until they surrender. The warden can then take back control of the prison."

Ezra stood up, "Let's go through the buffet line and get some food."

They had just gotten back with their food when one of Ezra's runners stepped into the room and whispered something to him. Ezra went over to his general, who was in the room, and asked the general to come with him. "Please excuse us. We need to go and check on a problem." He hesitated. "There is a large group of people threatening to storm the walls of our compound."

The visiting military general stood up and commented, "There was quite a large group of people out by the entrance gate when we came in a while ago. If my men and I can be of help, let me know."

"I will check on the problem and let you know," Ezra replied. The military general volunteered to go with him, and Ezra agreed. As they started to leave, they heard gunfire outside. They hurried out.

The military commander offered to drive them to the gate in his Jeep. When they arrived at the scene, they could see a group of Ezra's soldiers pointing their rifles at a large mob of people yelling and crowding the gate and fence to the compound. Some of the people in the mob had guns. One of Ezra's men had a megaphone and was trying to talk the mob into moving away from the compound.

The military's commanding general asked Ezra if he could have the megaphone. He exhibited confidence based on many years of experience. The crowd quieted some as this impressive-looking general stepped up beside his Humvee and cleared his throat.

"I am the commanding general of the military facility just outside of Atlanta. The military has decided to protect this community of people. We want you to know that the American government still exists, and so does the American military. We are making progress in dealing with this solar pulse. Eventually, everything the pulse destroyed will work again. We know that many people will starve and die before we can correct this, but you don't have to die today if you leave here now. We will shoot anyone trying to come over that fence. I repeat, the military will help defend this community. You must leave and live for another day."

The general stepped down from his Humvee and handed the megaphone to Ezra, who had stepped up to him.

Ezra called out, "I urge you to stop by our free water station as you leave. That is all we can offer you at this time. We assure you that the free water will continue to be available to you. Our snipers are watching the water site at all times to make sure that no one tries to take advantage of the water. Now, you must leave." Ezra stepped back, and his soldiers moved closer to the perimeter and fired shots into the air. The crowd quickly dispersed. Ezra looked at the general, saying, "Thank you for what you did! You just saved the day!"

The general answered, "I meant what I said about protecting your operation here. We can work together to establish several types of food production to maintain our future survival. Let's get back to our group and work on a plan. I would like to have this farmer from the Moline area join our planning."

As Ezra made his way back to his meeting room, he realized how close his community had been to being overrun by this large mob of starving people. He thought, "How important and timely is the military's offer to build a razor-wired topped fence around my community."

All the residents of Ezra's minimally walled area of protection were unaware of how close they had come to being overrun by this crowd of people. Ezra's soldiers would have killed a lot of them as they charged, but many would have broken in. This crowd was so large, looting would have devastated the food supplies in Ezra's compound. This starving mob would also have inflicted casualties on the residents.

John and Carol had decided that they would be safe if they stayed in Ezra's community. Today's events nearly proved that hope to be wrong.

Tom and his siblings were also unaware of how close they had been to getting raided by these starving people. Susie had voiced her concern earlier about how safe they might be while they were in Ezra's compound. She had hoped that their stay there would be short.

Chapter 23

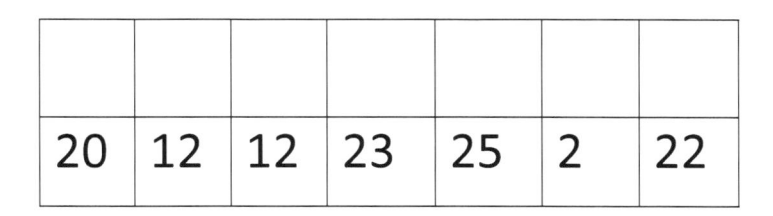

20	12	12	23	25	2	22

20	26	13	20

19	22	15	15	12		14	12	25

    David Billman, Tom, Benny, Mikey, and Barbie were finishing their breakfast when Ezra and the military commander came back into the restaurant. Ezra came over and asked if David and Tom would join them.

Benny announced that it was time for him, Mikey, and Barbie to go to class. On the way to school, Barbie talked about her fears of going home this afternoon because of the shooting.

When Ezra's group got to room four, they saw that all the others had gone to the buffet and gotten their food, so Ezra also took his people through the line. Tom and David got pastries and coffee to top off their meal. When they were all back and seated, Ezra announced, "The commander from the military was very helpful in dealing with the mob trying to storm our premises looking for food. I appreciate what he did. Now, David Billman and Tom, the commander wants you here because we want to prepare for the future survival of our country. David, there are many acres of good farmland where you live. We need to plan and develop different types of edible truck crops in quantity. The future survival of our country depends on establishing a reliable supply of eggs, poultry, pork, and beef. Our needs, in the beginning, have to be enough for everyone involved in re-establishing our country. That is a big order. We need enough in the small communities where the work is to be done for all the workers and their families. The military and their families and the government workers and their families must be considered.

"We are facing a tall order here. We will discuss this in more detail in a few minutes. First, let's start our plan for dealing with the prison gang. Commander, if you concur, I would like to have my general leave as soon as he finishes his meal and organize scouts to determine when the prison gang will all be back into the prison."

"Yes," the military commander quickly replied. "Let's get that in motion. I will get prepared to surround the prison and initiate a blockade to cut off their food and water supply. We will surround that place so they can never get back out."

Ezra's general responded, "It's urgent to deal with the prison gang issue because we have overheard chatter indicating they know where we are, and they are planning to come and get us." Having finished his meal, the general stood, put on his cap, and left.

The military commander proposed, "I can call my base and have a security unit sent here to start patrolling your boundaries. We have just finished building a wire wall with a razor wire at the top around the perimeter of our base and the family housing area next to the base. The military anticipates that there will be huge," and he emphasized 'huge,' "starving mobs from Atlanta trying to overrun any place that might appear to have food. We can now use these fence-building contractors supported by the US military to help secure strategic areas like yours. We could also build fencing in the Moline area if essential food production activities occur there. The military can also help with other aspects of production."

Ezra added, "We also have people who have researched how to acquire input needs. The kind of projects we're talking about will require seed stock from nurseries and seed companies. Fertilizer and machinery that will work will also be essential."

The military commander interrupted, "The government did some research on potential EMP pulse damage. They studied work on retrofitting damaged equipment. We can help, especially with the machinery needed for farming. We can help retrofit tillage tractors and harvesting equipment." The commander looked at David Billman and asked him what he thought about the farm produce potential where he lived.

David replied, "It's a good agricultural area. I raise mainly corn, wheat, and soybeans, but there are a lot of truck crops grown in the area, partly because of the closeness to the Atlanta markets. So, it is probably just a matter of finding the people who used to do it or finding people who want to grow these crops. I could raise some of these foods if I had the seeds and some training."

David paused, so Tom spoke up, "Right now is about the time that the Moline city council meets every day at Judy's bakery. I know that this group of people is very open to pursuing innovative ideas to help people survive this pulse. Commander, maybe we could get Judy on our ham radio, and you could tell the council what the US military wants in food-producing enterprises. This would get the council thinking about these projects. They know what has been done in their area. They also know the people who have been involved in these projects. The council could set up meetings for you with the people who know how to do the various projects."

"Yes, that would be extremely helpful." The commander thought a moment, then turned to Ezra. "Ezra, could you go with me to a meeting of this type, and we could plan together on getting the inputs required?"

Ezra smiled, "I would be glad to do that, and I would like to bring one or two of my researchers who know where resources are located. I can send some of my runners, my retired soldiers, with your military people if you could provide the transport and security to assure the inputs."

The commander smiled and replied, "That is exactly the kind of working together we need to make this thing successful."

Ezra had sent a runner to bring a ham radio. Tom dialed Judy's call number. He told the commander that Judy had done an excellent job at her food project of resurrecting an old bakery and getting it operating. "You probably cannot expect to get such good results in all the projects you try."

Judy answered, "Is this my ship captain? How is your visibility today?"

Tom laughed, "This lowly sailor is pretty serious today, Judy. I have a commander from the US military here at Ezra's. He would like to talk to you and the Moline city council about more potential food-producing enterprises."

Judy took Tom's message in stride. She replied, "I miss you too, Tom, but you have guessed right. The city council is here, and we would like to discuss new food-producing projects. I will take my ham radio in where the cinnamon rolls are. The council has circled around them."

Judy announced to the council that Tom and Ezra had a US military commander who wanted to talk to them about helping with new food-producing projects in the Moline area. "I will let the commander talk to our mayor, but first, I would like to tell you and Ezra we now have electricity and water here at the bakery and in much of Moline. We want to thank Ezra for that. Now, here is the mayor."

Chapter 24

7	19	22	25	26	23	22	20	20	8

26	9	22		25	9	12	16	22	13

The council took their seats, and the room became silent as the mayor and military commander began their conversation. "Commander, I don't know how to address you, but I like the sound of what you are interested in discussing."

"Mr. Mayor, I am impressed with Judy's report on your achievements there. We hope to help you achieve some more food-producing projects like what you have done with your bakery. I tasted some bread made from the flour you sent to Ezra. It was good; we would like to have some of it for the military. We can provide a military presence to protect the food-producing efforts in your area. We may want to send some government-employee families there to live in your relatively safe, small community. If you can get some potential producers lined up for us to meet, Ezra and I will come in person and visit with you. We can probably find the inputs needed to make a project work. Also, as I mentioned, we would provide security.

"I have just been made aware of a situation here that needs my attention. It was nice to talk briefly with you and your council, Mr. Mayor. Judy, keep up the good work and keep making those cinnamon rolls. I hope to taste one of them soon. We will be in touch."

Ezra's general came to give them an update on what his scouts were reporting. He told Ezra and the military commander that the prison gang members were returning to the prison as the evening approached. The military commander announced, "I need to make a call to have my units get ready to surround the prison."

After the commander made his call, he asked, "Do I understand that you have a grocery store here, Ezra?"

Ezra confirmed that he did, and he urged the commander and his men to take advantage of it before he left. Ezra invited them for lunch before they were to select their groceries. As they waited to hear from Ezra's scouts about the prison gang, it seemed like the time just ticked away so slowly. Ezra had sent out scouts all over Atlanta. They continued to report that the prison gang was returning to the prison.

Tom and David talked among themselves and with Ezra. They decided to leave in the morning if the prison gang was gone. Tom told Ezra that he wasn't sure that Benny and Susie would be as anxious to leave now as they had been at the start.

Ezra reminded Tom that he and the kids were welcome to stay. He also reminded Tom and David that large, hungry mobs were now forming and are something that we should consider in our plans to leave.

The military commander spoke to Ezra, "Ezra, if your scouts confirm that all of the prison gang returns to the prison tonight, call me, and we will surround the prison during the night."

Ezra answered him, "We will give you a call when we think they are all inside."

The commander and his men picked up the groceries they wanted and were ready to leave. Ezra asked him about the fence-building crew. The commander said, "Probably tomorrow."

Back in Huddersfield, England, the kids' grandmother awoke, startled. "I just had another scary dream about the kids. I have been so worried about them."

"What was this one about?" Grandpa Thomas asked.

"There were thousands of starving people looking over a fence. Their eyes were popping out, and their mouths were open. They had sharp teeth, and saliva was dripping from their mouths. This mob was looking at our grandkids sleeping peacefully, unaware of the danger they were in."

"It was just a dream, Grandma! You know people won't eat people," Grandpa consoled.

"Well, I can't help but worry as long as they are trapped in that huge city of Atlanta. I wish they were out of there!"

"You know that Peter and Martha told us that they will soon be getting out of there, and the kids have promised to call us when they do."

"I'm glad that Tom and Susie are keeping their parents informed of their situation. I worry so much about little Benny. Peter told us that a pack of starving dogs had attacked Benny. They said he was okay, but we don't know the story on that. I guess when they call, we will get the details. Our poor kids, they should have stayed here with us."

In Atlanta, Benny had gotten back from helping Dr. John. Mikey and Barbie finished class and came to where Tom and Benny were. They expressed a desire to leave the compound but were worried because of the large mob that was at the gate this morning. The commander heard them saying this, so he offered them a ride home. Mikey and Barbie were both excited to get a safe ride home. Benny hugged them both and told them that he would probably be leaving in the morning. Mikey whined, "You are the best friend I've ever had. You sure are the best mad-dog shooter I've ever seen."

Barbie hugged Benny and thanked him for saving their lives. "We sure are going to miss you, Benny." She asked, "Are you really going to start traveling in this crazy world? Are you going to try to bicycle all the way to Kansas?"

"Yes, we can do it if we stick together," Benny replied.

"I wish I was going with you," Mikey replied. "I'd have to get me a gun. I think going with you would be more fun than going to school."

Barbie admonished him by saying, "Now, Mikey, that sounds like a terribly scary adventure to me."

How To Decipher the Code

This simplistic code devised by Ezra's soldiers was a quick fix to deal with the prison gang. It is a simple backward alphabet corresponding to a forward numbering system. It was hoped that the prison gang could be quickly eliminated before they had time to decipher it.

Trapped in Atlanta

1	2	3	4	5	6	7	8	9	10
Z	Y	X	W	V	U	T	S	R	Q

11	12	13	14	15	16	17	18	19	20
P	O	N	M	L	K	J	I	H	G

21	22	23	24	25	26
F	E	D	C	B	A

R. Wesley Ibbetson

Coming Soon

Like a vulture, a helicopter circles overhead as the streets of Atlanta become consumed by starving people. Mystery packages, hostage situations, silence on the ham radio, premonitions of the doom and – Delubrum. R. Wesley Ibbetson will have you sitting on the edge of your seats in – Escape from Atlanta.

CONTENTS

1   WE ARE GOING HOME…………………………….7
2   GETTING OUT OF ATLANTA--OR NOT………...13
3   DELAYED AGAIN IN ATLANTA………………….20
4   JUDY'S BREAD………………………………………...27
5   MYSTERY PACKAGE……………………………….34
6   MYSTERY WOMAN………………………………...41
7   GRANDMA AND GRANDPA ROBINSON ………47
8   BART'S HOSTAGE…………………………………….54
9   JUDY'S FREE…………………………………………...61
10 BART THE PRISON GUARD………………………..68
11 JUDY ENJOYS EZRA'S PLACE……………………...75
12 TAKING GOOD CARE OF JUDY…………………..81
13 CONVOY OR FIRE AND BRIMSTONE……………88
14 REORGANIZED TO TRY AGAIN………………….95
15 THE REAL CONVOY……………………………….101
16 WELCOME BACK…………………………………..107
17 PREPARING TO TRAVEL………………………….113
18 THE ROUTE IS PLANNED……………………….119

19	CHATTANOOGA HERE WE COME	125
20	THE EGG PEOPLE	132
21	THE TRADERS	139
22	CHATTANOOGA	146
23	SCARFACE	153
24	TWO KIDS RESCUED	160
25	DELUBRUM	167
	COMING SOON, BOOK 5, DELUBRUM	176
	BOOK 5, CHAPTER 1, A BARN APPEARS IN THE SNOW	179
	BOOK 5, CHAPTER 2, DELUBRUM BARN MYSTERY	186

Book 4 Escape from Atlanta

Chapter 1

We Are Going Home

    The Robinson kids—Tom, Susie, and Benny—had been detained in Atlanta for a few weeks. The kids felt like the prison gang had captured them in Atlanta. They had been in a relatively safe and functioning community provided by a man they knew only by the name of Ezra. The rest of Atlanta was full of a starving and dying mass of people. The sun had produced a massive "EMP" pulse that destroyed much of the world's electronic technology. The city of Atlanta had shut down and turned off like most other cities around the world. There was no electricity, no automobiles, trains, or planes moving. No water pumps were working to provide water to the thirsty population of Atlanta. Trucks were not bringing food to restock the stores. There was no air conditioning during this hot early September. It had been a full month since the pulse hit.

The Robinson kids had been in England visiting their grandparents when they learned about the pulse coming. They had planned to fly home to their prepper-parents in Kansas and survive the apocalypse with them. They hoped to hide out on their farm until things returned to normal.

Tom, Susie, and Benny made it back to America, but the pulse hit as they crash-landed in Atlanta. Before they got out of the plane, they met a young lady about Tom's age named Judy. Judy invited them to go to her brother David's farm, 40 miles west of Atlanta. While at David's farm, the Robinson kids got a ham radio call from their dad asking them to go back into Atlanta to bring his brother and his wife out of that deteriorating city. Ezra had agreed to help get the kids' uncle, John, to his compound. Judy's brother, David, had a very old farm truck with no modern computer components, so the truck would still run. He and Tom agreed to take it into Atlanta and get Tom's uncle John and aunt Carol from Ezra's place.

Tom had insisted that Susie and Benny stay at the farm. He felt that it was too dangerous for them to go back into the city. Susie and Benny were not happy with Tom's plan. They stowed away in the back of the truckload of sacked grain and flour that was being taken to Ezra. It was a dangerous trip getting back into the Atlanta area. The prison gang attacked the truck. Susie emerged from the cargo and became a tail gunner in the back end of the truck. She shot a pursuing attacker and saved them from the attack.

All the Robinson kids ended up back in Atlanta together. They became trapped in Ezra's compound. The people who attacked them coming in were part of a very dangerous "prison gang" that had surfaced and was threatening all of Ezra's operations. It was unsafe for the Robinson kids and David Billman to return to his place.

Ezra and his retired soldiers worked on eliminating the prison gang. In the ensuing time, the Robinson kids and their uncle, Dr. John, and Aunt Carol became comfortable as they settled into the routine of living in Ezra's community. Finally, the military developed a solution to the prison gang problem. They were also interested in what Ezra was doing to re-establish some food-producing enterprises. With the prison gang eliminated by the military, the Robinson kids were suddenly looking at the possibility of getting out of Atlanta and getting back on their journey home.

This evening, Tom, Susie, and Benny gathered in their room with their ham radio. Benny urged Tom to hurry. "Come on, Tom. Get Mom and Dad on the radio so we can tell them the good news!"

"Hold your horses, Benny. I'm placing the call as fast as I can."

Their mother answered the kids' call and left in a hurry to get their dad, who was close by. As soon as they returned, Susie and Benny both shouted their good news.

"The prison gang is gone! We are planning to leave Atlanta in the morning. We are going to have a military escort."

Their dad broke in, "That's very good news! Why are you having a military escort if the prison gang is gone?"

Tom answered, "The military wants to send people to Moline to talk to the city council about food-producing projects. We will have several impressive military vehicles traveling with us. Ezra and some of his people are coming, too. The kids and I will go back with David Billman in his old farm truck."

Martha, the kids' mother, exclaimed, "It sounds like you should be safe getting out of Atlanta. I am thankful for that."

Peter, the kids' dad, asked, "What about John and his wife, Carol? Are they coming with you?"

The kids hesitated to answer, then Tom replied, "Uncle John and Carol have been very busy here. Ezra has security and safety and impressive medical facilities. Uncle John has a nearly full schedule all the time. He and Carol have apologized to us for risking our lives coming into Atlanta to get them. They now feel that they have an opportunity to fulfill their training here at Ezra's place. I think they should do this."

Susie agreed, "I think they should stay here. Ezra and these people need them."

Benny's weak voice agreed, "In a way, I wish we could stay here. I like Uncle John. He reminds me of you, Dad." Benny's sad voice trailed off.

Tom came to Benny's rescue, "Dad, Ezra has invited us to stay. It is nice here, and we all enjoy being around Uncle John and Aunt Carol. We may regret leaving. There have been times when we have felt that we should have stayed in Huddersfield, England, with our grandparents. I think all three of us are still in agreement to get on the road traveling back home to you."

"We want you kids back home with us," their mom exclaimed. "I hope that you can travel safely. We have talked to your grandparents on their ham radio, and they are worried sick about you."

Benny came back bravely, "We can do it, Mom. We just have to get past Tom's girlfriend in Moline. She'll want us to stay there."

Tom laughed, then paused, "It will be tempting to stay with Judy and our friends in the Moline area, but we have been making it clear to them that we plan to move on as soon as we can. So, Mom and Dad, we hope we can start moving a little bit in your direction tomorrow. We hope to get 40 miles closer to you. We will talk to you tomorrow."

Book 4 Escape from Atlanta

Chapter 2

Getting out of Atlanta—Or Not

David Billman, Tom, and some of Ezra's people got David's old farm truck fueled and ready to go the night before. They were all up early on departure day. David and the kids gathered one last time at the hidden restaurant where they had enjoyed so many meals.

Rachel was there, and she hugged Susie, saying, "I do wish you could all stay here with us. You would be safe here, and we would love to have you. I also know that your Uncle John and Aunt Carol would love to have you. We'll all miss you, but I also know that your parents would miss you even more if you were to stay."

John and Carol walked up at that moment, and Benny ran to his Uncle John and gave him a big hug. Benny blurted out, "We're going to head for Dad and Mom's place. I wish you were coming with us. We will miss you." Benny was all choked up. John and Carol both gave Benny a good hug; then, they hugged Susie and Tom.

John said, "We know you kids are determined to try to cross this country and get back home to your parents. So, all Carol and I can do is tell you again that we are sorry for getting you back into this danger in Atlanta. It looks like you can get out of here safely now. We hope and pray that all your travels go well and that you get back to your parents safely."

Ezra and Jacob arrived at that moment and came over to the Robinson's table. Ezra had a worried look on his face. When he got over to them, he cleared his throat and hesitated. "It may be a little early to be saying our goodbyes. I talked to the military commander this morning, and he has prepared a convoy of a fence-building crew and some trucks to travel to Moline with you. The convoy is encountering a large mass of people moving slowly southeast, apparently leaving the city. It is difficult to make any time traveling into that many people, but they will eventually get here. The convoy has the construction crew to build the razor wire fence around my community. It is important to get the fence built as soon as possible. The construction crew will move in and stay here until they finish. The commander said they sent up a helicopter to see where this mass of moving people blocked the roads."

Ezra paused and looked at the kids, "This mass of people has the road blocked that we want to take to Moline. The commander says we should delay our trip to Moline, and the military will concentrate on securing our community before we leave."

Tom moved over and put his arms around Susie and Benny. The news was obviously disappointing for them.

Susie looked toward Ezra and asked, "Where do all these people think they are going?"

"My runners tell me these Atlanta folks are starving to death, and they are hoping to find some food outside the city. They also know winter is coming. This mob has gotten the idea that they should travel toward Florida, where it will be warmer, and they can fish for food. This wave of people is ransacking all the grocery stores as they go, hoping to find something edible in these stores that hasn't already been taken."

Ezra paused, "It may take a few days for the streets to clear, and it is probably not a bad idea to get razor wire around my community before we leave. The fence crew can then go with us to the Moline area and start work there."

Susie and Benny looked at Tom with disappointment, wondering what they would do.

Susie voiced her concern to Tom, "What are we going to do, Tom?"

Tom quickly and confidently spoke in his usual calm and controlled voice, "No problem. We will just keep on doing what we have been doing for a few more days. You two have your jobs, and you can just keep on doing them. I will give Judy a quick call before she leaves for the Moline bakery and tell her about our delay."

Ezra heard Tom telling the kids he wanted to call Judy. "Tom, I would like to talk to Judy, also. Come with me; my ham radio is in the next room."

Tom agreed, "Okay. Susie, you and Benny, go ahead and get your food. I will be back soon."

Tom got Judy on Ezra's ham radio and broke the news. He had called the night before when they planned to leave early this morning.

Judy responded, "No! Am I ever going to get to see you again?"

"Oh yes, Judy. We will get through this. I am also disappointed about this delay. Ezra is here, and he would like to talk to you. Here he is."

"Hi, Judy! We're safe here partly due to the military. This situation is just a delay. Atlanta's going through the inevitable meltdown that we would expect in an apocalypse like this. As soon as the streets clear, we'll be heading your way. Please tell your city council that this is only temporary, but we want to meet with them as soon as we can get there. One new thing, we'll have a government fence building crew coming with us. You will need to feed and house this crew while they build fencing around the most vulnerable places. Your broiler and egg-laying buildings need to be protected. Potential truck crop areas need fencing around them. Talk to your council members about this. You may need an entire motel to house all of us for a while. Later, some government families may want to come there to live. The military will provide security.

"Oh yes, the military will want to load as much bread as you can spare. They will be sending trucks to transport the bread back to Atlanta. We will call you when we know we are heading your way."

Judy came back with a voice that sounded a little overwhelmed. "Thanks, Ezra… I think. I will talk to the council, and we will try to do our best."

"Good, I know you will, Judy, because you have proven that you can get the job done. We appreciate all that you are doing. I have to go, but I will let you talk to Tom. I know that he is missing you."

Ezra hurried off. Judy was suddenly back, more relaxed and confident. "Tom, are you there?"

"Yes, I'm here."

"Are you really missing me?"

Tom stuttered.

"That's not a yes," Judy blurted out. Tom finally got over Ezra's surprise introduction.

"Yes, Judy, I definitely am missing you. We are all disappointed about what happened this morning."

"But are you more disappointed than Susie and Benny?" Judy teased.

"Judy, I do miss you."

"Okay, Tom, I heard you. I know you would like to discuss missing me in more detail, but I need to leave for the bakery. It sounds like Ezra is sending the Army to carry off my bread. I hope to see you soon, but I know that our ships will only be passing in the night because you and the kids have made it very clear that you plan to get on the road home soon."

Chapter 7 ended with Susie talking to her grandmother. When an alarm went off where she was. Susie asked her grandma if she could call her back.

"Let me find out what it is. Hopefully it is not too serious."

Chapter 8

Bart's Hostage

Susie and the kids ended their ham radio call to their grandparents. Tom got up and headed out the door, saying, "I'm going to see if I can find out what is happening." The other kids followed him. They met Ezra and his general coming toward them.

Ezra addressed Tom, "We just got a call from one of the copter pilots coming from Moline. He says he is approaching to land and should have been here earlier. The pilot says a man with a gun is holding a woman hostage, and he wants to talk to you."

"What!" Tom yelled, "What's this about?"

"I will let you talk to the pilot. We are putting all our security people on alert."

Tom took Ezra's communications radio and nervously pressed the speaker button. "This is Tom Robinson, what is this about?"

"This is the pilot. I have a man here with a gun, and he is demanding to talk to a Tom Robinson."

"Okay," Tom replied, "Who is he, and why does he want to talk to me?"

"He says his name is Bart, and he says you owe him... you owe him something. I'm not sure what. He seems very angry."

"Oh, good grief, I do know him! But... was something said about a hostage?"

Previously in Moline, the government helicopter had not arrived in the morning on schedule. Later in the afternoon, the helicopter sound was heard in Moline. Both planes were arriving. One would take bread to the military base for the military and government officers living there. The other one would be taking bread to Ezra's community.

Somewhere in Moline, a couple of grungy-looking men had been dozing in the afternoon warmth. One of them awakened from the sound of the copters. He jerked awake with his eyes glaring. He yelled, "Let's go to the bakery."

His partner sleepily replied, "No, I'm tired. We were there this morning."

"I'm going; come on." The glary-eyed man stomped off. His sleepy-eyed partner reluctantly followed.

Judy jumped into hyper-mode when she heard the copters coming. They had not informed her that they would be coming off schedule like this, and she was short on help at this time of day. Judy immediately started stacking pallets of bread by the back door, ready to be loaded on the copters. She didn't have any dine-in customers at that time.

The two pilots met her at the back door as the front entrance door jingled. Judy didn't notice that somebody had come in from the street. The two of them stood briefly, waiting in the eating area. No one came to seat them, so one of them headed to the back room. Judy finally looked up and saw No-Way Bart standing there.

She exclaimed, "Bart! What are you doing here?"

"I came to help. It's about time that I take my rightful place with you. I started this whole emergency with you and that punk. I should be prospering right along with the rest of you. I am, we are," Bart looked at his partner, "we are going to help load those copters."

"Oh no you aren't! You have done too many wrong things in the past. I can't trust…."

"I didn't help steal your bikes! That was a misunderstanding. I deserve to be in this deal right along with you."

"No!" Judy slammed her fist into the palm of her other hand.

"Yes," retorted Bart, and he pulled out a gun from his pocket. Judy reached down and put her hand on her sidearm, but Bart shook his head. She removed her hand and raised both hands. Bart grabbed Judy and told the pilots to drop their weapons carefully. Bart told his sidekick to get their guns.

He whined, "I don't want to be a part of this."

"Do it now!" Bart waved his gun. The hesitant man proceeded to get the guns. The two pilots held their hands up and stood back in surprise. Bart screamed, "Get the copters loaded. My friend will help you. I will stay with my partner Judy and keep an eye on the operation."

Judy thought, "How did I let this happen again? I don't have any security here. I was here all by myself." The loading did not take long then Bart turned to Judy again.

"You and I are going to find your buddy, that young punk, what's his name...Tom Robinson. We're going to get an understanding that I'm part of this success story. I've been cheated out of everything all my life. You and I are getting on the copter that is going to wherever Punk is."

Bart's buddy, hearing that, yelled, "No, not me!" He bolted out the door. He still had the guns that he had collected.

Bart sneered, "Fine!" He waved his gun at Judy and the pilots. "Let's go!"

Back in Ezra's compound, Tom had asked the pilot about a hostage. The pilot answered, "It is a young lady. I think her name is Judy." Tom dropped the CB radio. Ezra bent over and picked it up. He looked at Tom, who was collecting his composure.

Ezra spoke to the pilot, "Ask the gunman if he will come inside and sit down and talk to Tom Robinson." The pilot checked, but Bart wanted Tom to come to the copter. Tom quickly agreed to do that.

When Tom got to the copter, he noticed that there was security surrounding it. He even saw some military soldiers that had been at the compound. Ezra had quickly gone on high alert. Tom climbed into the copter. He saw No-Way Bart standing with a gun on Judy, who was still seated. The pilot stepped out when Tom climbed in. Tom's eyes met Judy's. He was shaking inwardly, but Judy looked okay and seemed calm. She rolled her eyes as if she was totally irritated.

Tom's first question was to Judy. "Are you okay Judy?" She nodded.

Bart yelled, "Of course she's alright! I'm not going to hurt my partner. You know me, Punk. I'm just as good as any of you."

Tom instinctively started to call him No-Way, but he caught himself and addressed him as Bart. "Bart, I don't know you very well, but I assume you are as good as anybody. You know we do have that issue of you going with those thieves that stole Judy's bike."

"That was a mistake! They made me do it. We started in this mess together in the plane crash. You knew stuff, and you wouldn't include me. You knew what was happening, and you wouldn't tell me."

"Bart, what I remember was that I asked you if I could trade seats with you. I wanted to sit with my brother and sister and talk to our parents before the pulse killed our phones. We knew it was time for the pulse to hit."

"Yes, that's it! You knew, and you wouldn't tell me. I'm always left out."

"Bart, I was not trying to leave anyone out. I was just scared and was concerned about helping my sister and brother survive. I tended to ignore everyone that might slow down our survival prospects. You just happened to be one that didn't cooperate with my immediate survival plans. You even called me Punk. Otherwise, Bart I had nothing against you. In my mind you are as good as the next guy, but Bart, you have a gun on my... girlfriend, and if you didn't, I would try to help you."

Made in the USA
Columbia, SC
22 October 2023